Max and

with many more mischief-makers
more or less human or approximately animal

by
Wilhelm Busch

Edited and annotated by H. Arthur Klein

Translated by H. Arthur Klein and others

Dover Publications, Inc.
New York

This Dover edition, first published in 1962, is a
new selection of humorous pieces by Wilhelm
Busch. The English translations by H. Arthur
Klein and M. C. Klein and the Afterword by H.
Arthur Klein were especially prepared for this edition. The translation of "Max and Moritz" by C. T.
Brooks is an unabridged republication of the work
published by Roberts Brothers in 1871 under the
title *Max and Maurice*. "The Boy and the Popgun,"
"Ice-Peter" and "The Boy and the Pipe," translated
by Abby Langdon Alger, are reprinted in their
entirety from *The Mischief Book*, published by
R. Worthington in 1880.

International Standard Book Number: 0-486-20181-3
Library of Congress Catalog Card Number: 62-52768

Manufactured in the United States of America
Dover Publications, Inc.
180 Varick Street
New York, N.Y. 10014

To the youngsters nearest now—
David, and his neighbor-friends,
who happily in no way resemble
Max & Moritz or Paul & Peter:
    Tommy, Marga, Julie Kelsey, Stuart—
    Sharon, Kristen, Melissa, & Company.
May their futures all be fine
    & free from thermonuclear threats!

FOREWORD

As prelude to sadistic pranks:
The uttering of some heartfelt thanks ...

Duty, not stern but Heaven-sent,
This making of acknowledgement,
After the trial and tribulation
Of *zuverlässig-frei* translation!

But wherefor utter gratitudes
In stale, familiar platitudes?
Rather give voice to thoughts that tingle
In Busch-like bits of jaunty jingle. ...

My thanks are nearly running over
To Hayward Cirker, head of Dover,
For bringing out the book before us,
Named, as is meet, for *Max and Moritz,*
Together with a Busch-packed other,
A sister-volume (not a brother!)
Named for a certain wench—I mean a
Hypocritical Heléna...

Like this book, hers holds lots of stuff,
Some of it surely rough enough;
And things you'd hardly even think
Could happen, do—to folks who drink...

The two contain—no need to hush!—
A good bit of the best of Busch,
With more to come, should readers ask it,
Enough to fill a Busch–l basket!

And I, as double editor,
Must add one observation more:
It has indeed been no mean blessing
To have S. Appelbaum's "processing!"

Could books like these be finished, sans
The work of fine librarians?
By words alone can't be repaid
Helpful librarians' great aid!—

Deep thanks are due, I'm bound to say,
The Library of UCLA.

And great indeed's the debt I feel:
Good L.A. County Bookmobile!

My thanks sincere, not pert or witty:
The Library of L.A. City.

For book-loan lasting on and on,
Thanks—Bill and Fini Littlejohn!

It's fine to thank all, at the end—
Finest of all, to thank—one's friend!

Such thanks I send especially
To L.M. Linick, PhD;
Leroy, geschätzter Freund du bist
Ein königlicher Germanist!
Zu meinen Fragen, in der Tat,
Gabst du mir manchen weisen Rat,
So klipp und klar und immer-treffend,
Es war und bleibt mir fast verblüffend!

Mein Dank, wie immer, schliesset ein
Meine eig'ne Frau, die "M. C. Klein!"
Nicht länger woll'n wir hier aufhalten;
Lass' nun die bösen Buben walten!

    Sagt dazu niemals, "Es soll nicht sein!"
    So ratet euch

        —H. Arthur Klein
        (Herausgeber)

CONTENTS

Major Mischief-makers:

The Terrible Twosomes

I

MAX AND MORITZ

A Juvenile History in Seven Tricks

(Max und Moritz:

Eine Bubengeschichte in sieben Streichen)

Translated by Charles T. Brooks

Preface	Vorwort
Ah, how oft we read or hear of Boys we almost stand in fear of! For example, take these stories	Ach, was muß man oft von bösen Kindern hören oder lesen!! Wie zum Beispiel hier von diesen,

Of two youths, named Max and Moritz,	Welche Max und Moritz hießen;
Who, instead of early turning Their young minds to useful learning, Often leered with horrid features At their lessons and their teachers. Look now at the empty head: he Is for mischief always ready. Teasing creatures, climbing fences, Stealing apples, pears, and quinces, Is, of course, a deal more pleasant, And far easier for the present, Than to sit in schools or churches, Fixed like roosters on their perches. But O dear, O dear, O deary, When the end comes sad and dreary! 'Tis a dreadful thing to tell That on Max and Moritz fell! All they did this book rehearses, Both in pictures and in verses.	Die, anstatt durch weise Lehren Sich zum Guten zu bekehren, Oftmals noch darüber lachten Und sich heimlich lustig machten. – – Ja, zur Übeltätigkeit, Ja, dazu ist man bereit! – – Menschen necken, Tiere quälen, Äpfel, Birnen, Zwetschgen stehlen – – Das ist freilich angenehmer Und dazu auch viel bequemer, Als in Kirche oder Schule Festzusitzen auf dem Stuhle. – Aber wehe, wehe, wehe! Wenn ich auf das Ende sehe!! – – Ach, das war ein schlimmes Ding, Wie es Max und Moritz ging! – Drum ist hier, was sie getrieben, Abgemalt und aufgeschrieben.

Max and Moritz

First Trick	Erster Streich
To most people who have leisure	Mancher gibt sich viele Müh'
Raising poultry gives great	Mit dem lieben Federvieh;
pleasure:	Einesteils der Eier wegen,
First, because the eggs they lay us	Welche diese Vögel legen;
For the care we take repay us;	Zweitens: weil man dann und wann
Secondly, that now and then	Einen Braten essen kann;
We can dine on roasted hen;	Drittens aber nimmt man auch
Thirdly, of the hen's and goose's	Ihre Federn zum Gebrauch
Feathers men make various uses.	In die Kissen und die Pfühle,
Some folks like to rest their heads	Denn man liegt nicht gerne
In the night on feather beds.	kühle. –

One of these was Widow Tibbets,	Seht, da ist die Witwe Bolte,
Whom the cut you see exhibits.	Die das auch nicht gerne wollte.

Hens were hers in number three,	Ihrer Hühner waren drei
And a cock of majesty.	Und ein stolzer Hahn dabei. –

Max und Moritz

Max and Moritz took a view;	Max und Moritz dachten nun:
Fell to thinking what to do.	Was ist hier jetzt wohl zu tun? –
One, two, three! as soon as said,	– Ganz geschwinde, eins, zwei, drei,
They have sliced a loaf of bread,	Schneiden sie sich Brot entzwei,

Cut each piece again in four,	In vier Teile, jedes Stück
Each a finger thick, no more.	Wie ein kleiner Finger dick.
These to two cross-threads they tie,	Diese binden sie an Fäden,
Like a letter X they lie	Übers Kreuz, ein Stück an jeden,
In the widow's yard, with care	Und verlegen sie genau
Stretched by those two rascals there.	In den Hof der guten Frau. –
Scarce the cock had seen the sight,	Kaum hat dies der Hahn gesehen,
When he up and crew with might:	Fängt er auch schon an zu krähen:

Cock-a-doodle-doodle-doo;—	Kikeriki! Kikikerikih!! –
Tack, tack, tack, the trio flew.	Tak, tak, tak! – da kommen sie.

Cock and hens, like fowls unfed,
Gobbled each a piece of bread;

Hahn und Hühner schlucken
    munter
Jedes ein Stück Brot hinunter;

But they found, on taking thought,
Each of them was badly caught.

Aber als sie sich besinnen,
Konnte keines recht von hinnen.

Max und Moritz

Every way they pull and twitch, This strange cat's-cradle to unhitch;	In die Kreuz und in die Quer Reißen sie sich hin und her,

Up into the air they fly, Jiminee, O Jimini!	Flattern auf und in die Höh', Ach herrje, herrjemine!

On a tree behold them dangling,
In the agony of strangling!
And their necks grow long and
   longer,
And their groans grow strong and
   stronger.

Ach, sie bleiben an dem langen,
Dürren Ast des Baumes hangen. –
– Und ihr Hals wird lang und
   länger,
Ihr Gesang wird bang und bänger.

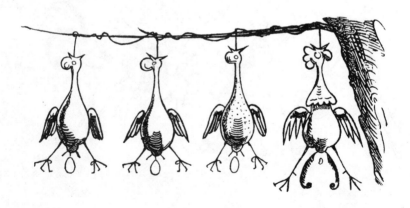

Each lays quickly one egg more,
Then they cross to th' other shore.

Jedes legt noch schnell ein Ei,
Und dann kommt der Tod herbei.

| Widow Tibbets in her chamber, | Witwe Bolte in der Kammer |
| By these death-cries waked from slumber, | Hört im Bette diesen Jammer; |

| Rushes out with bodeful thought: | Ahnungsvoll tritt sie heraus: |
| Heavens! what sight her vision caught! | Ach, was war das für ein Graus! |

From her eyes the tears are
  streaming:
"Oh, my cares, my toil, my
  dreaming!
Ah, life's fairest hope," says she,
"Hangs upon that apple-tree."

„Fließet aus dem Aug', ihr
  Tränen!
All mein Hoffen, all mein Sehnen,
Meines Lebens schönster Traum
Hängt an diesem Apfelbaum!!"

Heart-sick (you may well suppose),
For the carving-knife she goes;
Cuts the bodies from the bough,
Hanging cold and lifeless now;

Tiefbetrübt und sorgenschwer
Kriegt sie jetzt das Messer her;
Nimmt die Toten von den Strängen,
Daß sie so nicht länger hängen,

And in silence, bathed in tears,
Through her house-door disappears.

Und mit stummem Trauerblick
Kehrt sie in ihr Haus zurück. –

This was the bad boys' first trick,
But the second follows quick.

Dieses war der erste Streich,
Doch der zweite folgt sogleich.

Second Trick

When the worthy Widow Tibbets
(Whom the cut below exhibits)
Had recovered, on the morrow,
From the dreadful shock of sorrow,
She (as soon as grief would let her
Think) began to think 'twere better
Just to take the dead, the dear ones
(Who in life were walking here
  once),
And in a still noonday hour
Them, well roasted, to devour.
True, it did seem almost wicked,
When they lay so bare and naked,
Picked, and singed before the
  blaze,—
They that once in happier days,
In the yard or garden ground,
All day long went scratching
  round.

Zweiter Streich

Als die gute Witwe Bolte
Sich von ihrem Schmerz erholte,
Dachte sie so hin und her,
Daß es wohl das beste wär',
Die Verstorb'nen, die hienieden
Schon so frühe abgeschieden,
Ganz im stillen und in Ehren
Gut gebraten zu verzehren. –
– Freilich war die Trauer groß,
Als sie nun so nackt und bloß
Abgerupft am Herde lagen,
Sie, die einst in schönen Tagen
Bald im Hofe, bald im Garten
Lebensfroh im Sande scharrten. –

Ah! Frau Tibbets wept anew,
And poor Spitz was with her, too.

Ach, Frau Bolte weint aufs neu,
Und der Spitz steht auch dabei. –

Max and Moritz smelt the savor.
"Climb the roof!" cried each young
  shaver.

Max und Moritz rochen dieses;
,,Schnell aufs Dach gekrochen!"
  hieß es.

Through the chimney now, with
  pleasure,
They behold the tempting treasure,
Headless, in the pan there, lying,
Hissing, browning, steaming, frying.

Durch den Schornstein mit
  Vergnügen
Sehen sie die Hühner liegen,
Die schon ohne Kopf und Gurgeln
Lieblich in der Pfanne
  schmurgeln. –

Max and Moritz

At that moment down the cellar　Eben geht mit einem Teller
(Dreaming not what soon befell her)　Witwe Bolte in den Keller,

Widow Tibbets went for sour　Daß sie von dem Sauerkohle
Krout, which she would oft devour　Eine Portion sich hole,
With exceeding great desire　Wofür sie besonders schwärmt,
(Warmed a little at the fire).　Wenn er wieder aufgewärmt. –

Up there on the roof, meanwhile,　– Unterdessen auf dem Dache
They are doing things in style.　Ist man tätig bei der Sache.
Max already with forethought　Max hat schon mit Vorbedacht
A long fishing-line has brought.　Eine Angel mitgebracht.

14

Max und Moritz

Schnupdiwup! there goes, O
    Jeminy!
One hen dangling up the chimney.

Schnupdiwup! da wird nach oben
Schon ein Huhn heraufgehoben.

Schnupdiwup! a second bird!
Schnupdiwup! up comes the third!
Presto! number four they haul!
Schnupdiwup! we have them all!—
Spitz looks on, we must allow,
But he barks: Row-wow! Row-
  wow!

Schnupdiwup! jetzt Numro zwei;
Schnupdiwup! jetzt Numro drei;
Und jetzt kommt noch Numro vier:
Schnupdiwup! dich haben wir!! –
Zwar der Spitz sah es genau,
Und er bellt: Rawau! Rawau!

But the rogues are down instanter
From the roof, and off they
  canter.—

Aber schon sind sie ganz munter
Fort und von dem Dach
  herunter. –

Ha! I guess there'll be a humming;
Here's the Widow Tibbets coming!
Rooted stood she to the spot,
When the pan her vision caught.

– Na! Das wird Spektakel geben,
Denn Frau Bolte kommt soeben;
Angewurzelt stand sie da,
Als sie nach der Pfanne sah.

Gone was every blessed bird!
"Horrid Spitz!" was her first word.

Alle Hühner waren fort –
„Spitz!!" – das war ihr erstes
Wort. –

"O you Spitz, you monster, you!
Let me beat him black and blue!"
And the heavy ladle, thwack!
Comes down on poor Spitz's back!

„Oh, du Spitz, du Ungetüm!!
Aber wart! ich komme ihm!!!"
Mit dem Löffel, groß und schwer,
Geht es über Spitzen her;

| Loud he yells with agony, | Laut ertönt sein Wehgeschrei, |
| For he feels his conscience free. | Denn er fühlt sich schuldenfrei. – |

Max and Moritz, dinner over,	– Max und Moritz im Verstecke
In a hedge, snored under cover;	Schnarchen aber an der Hecke
And of that great hen-feast now	Und vom ganzen Hühnerschmaus
Each has but a leg to show.	Guckt nur noch ein Bein heraus.

| This was now the second trick, | Dieses war der zweite Streich, |
| But the third will follow quick. | Doch der dritte folgt sogleich. |

18

Third Trick

Through the town and country
   round
Was one Mr. Buck renowned.

Dritter Streich

Jedermann im Dorfe kannte
Einen, der sich Böck benannte. –

Sunday coats, and week-day sack-
   coats,
Bob-tails, swallow-tails, and frock
   coats,
Gaiters, breeches, hunting-jackets;
Waistcoats, with commodious
   pockets,—
And other things, too long to
   mention,
Claimed Mr. Tailor Buck's
   attention.
Or, if any thing wanted doing
In the way of darning, sewing,
Piecing, patching,—if a button
Needed to be fixed or put on,—
Any thing of any kind,
Anywhere, before, behind,—
Master Buck could do the same,
For it was his life's great aim.
Therefore all the population
Held him high in estimation.
Max and Moritz tried to invent
Ways to plague this worthy gent.

– Alltagsröcke, Sonntagsröcke,
Lange Hosen, spitze Fräcke,
Westen mit bequemen Taschen,
Warme Mäntel und Gamaschen –
Alle diese Kleidungssachen
Wußte Schneider Böck zu
   machen. –
Oder wäre was zu flicken,
Abzuschneiden, anzustücken,
Oder gar ein Knopf der Hose
Abgerissen oder lose –
Wie und wo und was es sei,
Hinten, vorne, einerlei –
Alles macht der Meister Böck,
Denn das ist sein Lebenszweck. –
– Drum so hat in der Gemeinde
Jedermann ihn gern zum
   Freunde. –
– Aber Max und Moritz dachten,
Wie sie ihn verdrießlich
   machten. –

Right before the Sartor's dwelling
Ran a swift stream, roaring,
  swelling.

Nämlich vor des Meisters Hause
Floß ein Wasser mit Gebrause.

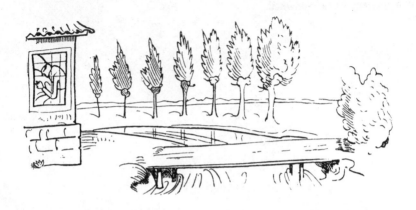

This swift stream a bridge did span,
And the road across it ran.

Übers Wasser führt ein Steg
Und darüber geht der Weg. –

Max and Moritz (naught could awe
  them!)
Took a saw, when no one saw
  them:
Ritze-ratze! riddle-diddle!
Sawed a gap across the middle.

Max und Moritz, gar nicht träge,
Sägen heimlich mit der Säge,
Ritzeratze! voller Tücke,
In die Brücke eine Lücke. –

Max und Moritz

When this feat was finished well,
Suddenly was heard a yell:

Als nun diese Tat vorbei,
Hört man plötzlich ein Geschrei:

"Hallo, there! Come out, you buck!
Tailor, Tailor, muck! muck!
  muck!"
Buck could bear all sorts of jeering,
Jibes and jokes in silence hearing;
But this insult roused such anger,
Nature couldn't stand it longer.

,,He, heraus! du Ziegen-Böck!
Schneider, Schneider, meck, meck,
  meck!!" –
– Alles konnte Böck ertragen,
Ohne nur ein Wort zu sagen;
Aber wenn er dies erfuhr,
Ging's ihm wider die Natur.

Wild with fury, up he started,
With his yard-stick out he darted;
For once more that frightful jeer,
"Muck! muck! muck!" rang loud
  and clear.

Schnelle springt er mit der Elle
Über seines Hauses Schwelle,
Denn schon wieder ihm zum
  Schreck
Tönt ein lautes: ,,Meck, meck,
  meck!!"

On the bridge one leap he makes;
Crash! beneath his weight it breaks.

Und schon ist er auf der Brücke,
Kracks! die Brücke bricht in
Stücke;

Once more rings the cry, "Muck!
muck!"
In, headforemost, plumps poor
Buck!

Wieder tönt es: ,,Meck, meck,
meck!"
Plumps! Da ist der Schneider weg!

While the scared boys were skedaddling,
Down the brook two geese came paddling.
On the legs of these two geese,
With a death-clutch, Buck did seize;

Grad als dieses vorgekommen,
Kommt ein Gänsepaar geschwommen,
Welches Böck in Todeshast
Krampfhaft bei den Beinen faßt.

And, with both geese *well in hand*,
Flutters out upon dry land.

Beide Gänse in der Hand,
Flattert er auf trocknes Land. –

For the rest he did not find
Things exactly to his mind.

Übrigens bei alledem
Ist so etwas nicht bequem;

Soon it proved poor Buck had
brought a
Dreadful belly-ache from the water.

Wie denn Böck von der Geschichte
Auch das Magendrücken kriegte.

Max und Moritz

Noble Mrs. Buck! She rises Fully equal to the crisis; With a hot flat-iron, she Draws the cold out famously.	Hoch ist hier Frau Böck zu preisen! Denn ein heißes Bügeleisen, Auf den kalten Leib gebracht, Hat es wieder gut gemacht. –

Soon 'twas in the mouths of men, All through town: "Buck's up again!"	– Bald im Dorf hinauf, hinunter, Hieß es: Böck ist wieder munter!!
This was the bad boys' third trick, But the fourth will follow quick.	Dieses war der dritte Streich, Doch der vierte folgt sogleich.

Fourth Trick

An old saw runs somewhat so:
Man must learn while here below.—
Not alone the A, B, C,
Raises man in dignity;
Not alone in reading, writing,
Reason finds a work inviting;
Not alone to solve the double
Rule of Three shall man take
   trouble;
But must hear with pleasure Sages
Teach the wisdom of the ages.

Vierter Streich

Also lautet ein Beschluß:
Daß der Mensch was lernen muß. –
– Nicht allein das A-B-C
Bringt den Menschen in die Höh';
Nicht allein im Schreiben, Lesen
Übt sich ein vernünftig Wesen;
Nicht allein in Rechnungssachen
Soll der Mensch sich Mühe machen;
Sondern auch der Weisheit Lehren
Muß man mit Vergnügen hören. –

Of this wisdom an example
To the world was Master Lämpel.

Daß dies mit Verstand geschah,
War Herr Lehrer Lämpel da. –

For this cause, to Max and Moritz
This man was the chief of horrors;
For a boy who loves bad tricks
Wisdom's friendship never seeks.

– Max und Moritz, diese beiden,
Mochten ihn darum nicht leiden;
Denn wer böse Streiche macht,
Gibt nicht auf den Lehrer acht. –

Max und Moritz

With the clerical profession
Smoking always was a passion;
And this habit without question,
While it helps promote digestion,
Is a comfort no one can
Well begrudge a good old man,
When the day's vexations close,
And he sits to seek repose.—

Nun war dieser brave Lehrer
Von dem Tobak ein Verehrer,
Was man ohne alle Frage
Nach des Tages Müh und Plage
Einem guten, alten Mann
Auch von Herzen gönnen kann. –

Max and Moritz, flinty-hearted,
On another trick have started;
Thinking how they may attack a
Poor old man through his tobacco.

– Max und Moritz, unverdrossen,
Sinnen aber schon auf Possen,
Ob vermittelst seiner Pfeifen
Dieser Mann nicht anzugreifen. –

Once, when Sunday morning
    breaking,
Pious hearts to gladness waking,

– Einstens, als es Sonntag wieder
Und Herr Lämpel brav und bieder

Poured its light where, in the
    temple,
At his organ sate Herr Lämpel,

In der Kirche mit Gefühle
Saß vor seinem Orgelspiele,

Max and Moritz

These bad boys, for mischief ready,
Stole into the good man's study,
Where his darling meerschaum
   stands.
This, Max holds in both his hands;

Schlichen sich die bösen Buben
In sein Haus und seine Stuben,
Wo die Meerschaumpfeife stand;
Max hält sie in seiner Hand;

While young Moritz (scapegrace
   born!)
Climbs, and gets the powderhorn,
And with speed the wicked soul
Pours the powder in the bowl.
Hush, and quick! now, right about!
For already church is out.

Aber Moritz aus der Tasche
Zieht die Flintenpulverflasche,
Und geschwinde, stopf, stopf,
   stopf!
Pulver in den Pfeifenkopf. –
Jetzt nur still und schnell nach
   Haus,
Denn schon ist die Kirche aus. –

Lämpel closes the church-door,
Glad to seek his home once more;

– Eben schließt in sanfter Ruh'
Lämpel seine Kirche zu;

All his service well got through,
Takes his keys, and music too,

Und mit Buch und Notenheften,
Nach besorgten Amtsgeschäften,

And his way, delighted, wends
Homeward to his silent friends.

Lenkt er freudig seine Schritte
Zu der heimatlichen Hütte,

Full of gratitude he there
Lights his pipe, and takes his chair.

Und voll Dankbarkeit sodann,
Zündet er sein Pfeifchen an.

"Ah!" he says, "no joy is found
Like contentment on earth's
round!"

,,Ach!" – spricht er – ,,die
größte Freud'
Ist doch die Zufriedenheit!! –"

Fizz! whizz! bum! The pipe is
burst,
Almost shattered into dust.
Coffee-pot and water-jug,
Snuff-box, ink-stand, tumbler, mug,
Table, stove, and easy-chair,
All are flying through the air
In a lightning-powder-flash,
With a most tremendous crash.

Rums!! – Da geht die Pfeife los
Mit Getöse, schrecklich groß.
Kaffeetopf und Wasserglas,
Tobaksdose, Tintenfaß,
Ofen, Tisch und Sorgensitz
Alles fliegt im Pulverblitz. –

When the smoke-cloud lifts and
   clears,
Lämpel on his back appears;
God be praised! still breathing
   there,
Only somewhat worse for wear.

Als der Dampf sich nun erhob,
Sieht man Lämpel, der – gottlob!
Lebend auf dem Rücken liegt;
Doch er hat was abgekriegt.

Nose, hands, eyebrows (once like
   yours),
Now are black as any Moor's;
Burned the last thin spear of hair,
And his pate is wholly bare.

Nase, Hand, Gesicht und Ohren
Sind so schwarz als wie die Mohren,
Und des Haares letzter Schopf
Ist verbrannt bis auf den Kopf. –

31

Who shall now the children guide,
Lead their steps to wisdom's side?
Who shall now for Master Lämpel
Lead the service in the temple?
Now that his old pipe is out,
Shattered, smashed, *gone up the
  spout*?

Wer soll nun die Kinder lehren
Und die Wissenschaft vermehren?
Wer soll nun für Lämpel leiten
Seine Amtestätigkeiten?
Woraus soll der Lehrer rauchen,
Wenn die Pfeife nicht zu
  brauchen??

Time will heal the rest once more,
But the pipe's best days are o'er.

Mit der Zeit wird alles heil,
Nur die Pfeife hat ihr Teil.

This was the bad boys' fourth trick,
But the fifth will follow quick.

Dieses war der vierte Streich,
Doch der fünfte folgt sogleich.

Fifth Trick

If, in village or in town,
You've an uncle settled down,
Always treat him courteously;
Uncle will be pleased thereby.
In the morning: "Morning to you!
Any errand I can do you?"
Fetch whatever he may need,—
Pipe to smoke, and news to read;
Or should some confounded thing
Prick his back, or bite, or sting,
Nephew then will be near by,
Ready to his help to fly;
Or a pinch of snuff, maybe,
Sets him sneezing violently:
"Prosit! uncle! good health to you!
God be praised! much good may't
   do you!"
Or he comes home late, perchance:
Pull his boots off then at once,
Fetch his slippers and his cap,
And warm gown his limbs to wrap.
Be your constant care, good boy,
What shall give your uncle joy.

Max and Moritz (need I mention?)
Had not any such intention.
See now how they tried their wits—
These bad boys—on Uncle Fritz.

Fünfter Streich

Wer im Dorfe oder Stadt
Einen Onkel wohnen hat,
Der sei höflich und bescheiden,
Denn das mag der Onkel leiden. –
– Morgens sagt man: „Guten
   Morgen!
Haben Sie was zu besorgen?"
Bringt ihm, was er haben muß:
Zeitung, Pfeife, Fidibus. –
Oder sollt' es wo im Rücken
Drücken, beißen oder zwicken,
Gleich ist man mit Freudigkeit
Dienstbeflissen und bereit. –
Oder sei's nach einer Prise,
Daß der Onkel heftig niese,
Ruft man: „Prosit!" allsogleich,
„Danke, wohl bekomm' es
   Euch!"
Oder kommt er spät nach Haus,
Zieht man ihm die Stiefel aus,
Holt Pantoffel, Schlafrock, Mütze,
Daß er nicht im Kalten sitze –
Kurz, man ist darauf bedacht,
Was dem Onkel Freude macht. –

– Max und Moritz ihrerseits
Fanden darin keinen Reiz. –
– Denkt euch nur, welch'
   schlechten Witz
Machten sie mit Onkel Fritz! –

Max and Moritz

What kind of a bird a May-
Bug was, *they* knew, I dare say;
In the trees they may be found,
Flying, crawling, wriggling round.

Jeder weiß, was so ein Mai-
Käfer für ein Vogel sei.
In den Bäumen hin und her
Fliegt und kriecht und krabbelt
    er.

Max and Moritz, great pains taking,
From a tree these bugs are shaking.

Max und Moritz, immer munter,
Schütteln sie vom Baum herunter.

Max und Moritz

In their cornucopiae papers,
They collect these pinching creepers.

In die Tüte von Papiere
Sperren sie die Krabbeltiere. –

Soon they are deposited
In the foot of uncle's bed!

Fort damit, und in die Ecke
Unter Onkel Fritzens Decke!

With his peaked nightcap on,
Uncle Fritz to bed has gone;

Bald zu Bett geht Onkel Fritze
In der spitzen Zippelmütze;

Tucks the clothes in, shuts his eyes,
And in sweetest slumber lies.

Seine Augen macht er zu,
Hüllt sich ein und schläft in Ruh.

| Kritze! Kratze! come the Tartars
Single file from their night quarters. | Doch die Käfer, kritze, kratze!
Kommen schnell aus der Matratze. |

| And the captain boldly goes
Straight at Uncle Fritzy's nose. | Schon faßt einer, der voran,
Onkel Fritzens Nase an. |

"Baugh!" he cries: "what have we here?" Seizing that grim grenadier.	,,Bau!!" schreit er – ,,Was ist das hier?!!" Und erfaßt das Ungetier.

Uncle, wild with fright, upspringeth, And the bedclothes from him flingeth.	Und den Onkel, voller Grausen, Sieht man aus dem Bette sausen.

"Awtsch!" he seizes two more scape-
Graces from his shin and nape.

,,Autsch!!" – Schon wieder hat er einen
Im Genicke, an den Beinen;

Crawling, flying, to and fro,
Round the buzzing rascals go.

Hin und her und rund herum
Kriecht es, fliegt es mit Gebrumm.

Max and Moritz

Wild with fury, Uncle Fritz
Stamps and slashes them to bits.

Onkel Fritz, in dieser Not,
Haut und trampelt alles tot.

O be joyful! all gone by
Is the May bug's deviltry.

Guckste wohl! Jetzt ist's vorbei
Mit der Käferkrabbelei!!

40

Max und Moritz

Uncle Fritz his eyes can close
Once again in sweet repose.

Onkel Fritz hat wieder Ruh'
Und macht seine Augen zu.

This was the bad boys' fifth trick,
But the sixth will follow quick.

Dieses war der fünfte Streich,
Doch der sechste folgt sogleich.

Easter days have come again,
When the pious baker men
Bake all sorts of sugar things,
Plum-cakes, ginger-cakes, and
   rings.
Max and Moritz feel an ache
In their sweet-tooth for some cake.

In der schönen Osterzeit,
Wenn die frommen Bäckersleut'
Viele süße Zuckersachen
Backen und zurechte machen,
Wünschten Max und Moritz auch
Sich so etwas zum Gebrauch. –

But the Baker thoughtfully
Locks his shop, and takes the key.

Doch der Bäcker, mit Bedacht,
Hat das Backhaus zugemacht.

Who would steal, then, *this* must
  do:
Wriggle down the chimney-flue.

Also, will hier einer stehlen,
Muß er durch den Schlot sich
  quälen.

Ratsch! There come the boys, my
    Jiminy!
Black as ravens, down the chimney.

Ratsch!! – Da kommen die zwei
    Knaben
Durch den Schornstein, schwarz
    wie Raben.

Puff! into a chest they drop,
Full of flour up to the top.

Puff! – Sie fallen in die Kist',
Wo das Mehl darinnen ist.

Max und Moritz

Out they crawl from under cover
Just as white as chalk all over.

Da! Nun sind sie alle beide
Rund herum so weiß wie Kreide.

But the cracknels, precious
  treasure,
On a shelf they spy with pleasure.

Aber schon mit viel Vergnügen
Sehen sie die Brezeln liegen.

45

Max and Moritz

Knacks! The chair breaks! down they go—

Knacks!! – Da bricht der Stuhl entzwei.

Schwapp!—into a trough of dough!

Schwapp!! – Da liegen sie im Brei.

All enveloped now in dough,
See them, monuments of woe.

Ganz von Kuchenteig umhüllt
Stehn sie da als Jammerbild. –

In the Baker comes, and snickers
When he sees the sugar-lickers.

Gleich erscheint der Meister Bäcker
Und bemerkt die Zuckerlecker.

One, two, three! the brats, behold!
Into two good *brots* are rolled.

Eins, zwei, drei! – eh' man's
    gedacht,
Sind zwei Brote draus gemacht.

There's the oven, all red-hot,—
Shove 'em in as quick as thought.

In dem Ofen glüht es noch
Ruff!! – damit ins Ofenloch!

Ruff! out with 'em from the heat,
They are brown and good to eat.

Ruff!! Man zieht sie aus der Glut;
Denn nun sind sie braun und gut. –

Now you think they've *paid the debt!*
No, my friend, they're living yet.

– Jeder denkt, „die sind perdü!"
Aber nein! – noch leben sie! –

Knusper! Knasper! like two mice
Through their roofs they gnaw in a
    trice;

Knusper, knasper! – Wie zwei
    Mäuse
Fressen sie durch das Gehäuse;

And the Baker cries, "You bet!
There's the rascals living yet!"

Und der Meister Bäcker schrie:
„Ach herrje! da laufen sie!!" –

This was the bad boys' sixth trick,
But the last will follow quick.

Dieses war der sechste Streich,
Doch der letzte folgt sogleich.

Last Trick	Letzter Streich
Max and Moritz! I grow sick,	Max und Moritz, wehe euch!
When I think on your last trick.	Jetzt kommt euer letzter Streich! –

Why must these two scalawags	Wozu müssen auch die beiden
Cut those gashes in the bags?	Löcher in die Säcke schneiden?? –

See! the farmer on his back	– Seht, da trägt der Bauer Mecke
Carries corn off in a sack.	Einen seiner Maltersäcke. –

Scarce has he begun to travel,
When the corn runs out like gravel.

Aber kaum, daß er von hinnen,
Fängt das Korn schon an zu rinnen.

All at once he stops and cries:
"Darn it! I see where it lies!"

Und verwundert steht und spricht er:
„Zapperment! Dat Ding werd lichter!"

Max und Moritz

Ha! with what delighted eyes
Max and Moritz he espies.

Hei! Da sieht er voller Freude
Max und Moritz im Getreide.

Rabs! he opens wide his sack,
Shoves the rogues in—Hukepack!

Rabs!! – In seinen großen Sack
Schaufelt er das Lumpenpack.

53

Max and Moritz

It grows warm with Max and
   Moritz,
For to mill the farmer hurries.

Max und Moritz wird es schwüle,
Denn nun geht es nach der
   Mühle. –

"Master Miller! Hallo, man!
Grind me *that* as quick as you can!"

,,Meister Müller, he, heran!
Mahl' er das, so schnell er kann!"

"In with 'em!" Each wretched
  flopper
Headlong goes into the hopper.

,,Her damit!!" Und in den Trichter
Schüttelt er die Bösewichter. –

As the farmer turns his back, he
Hears the mill go "creaky!
  cracky!"

Rickeracke! Rickeracke!
Geht die Mühle mit Geknacke.

Here you see the bits *post mortem*,
Just as Fate was pleased to sort
'em.

Hier kann man sie noch erblicken
Fein geschroten und in Stücken.

Master Miller's ducks with speed

Doch sogleich verzehret sie

Gobbled up the coarse-grained feed.

Meister Müllers Federvieh.

56

In the village not a word,
Not a sign, of grief, was heard.
Widow Tibbets, speaking low,
Said, "I thought it would be so!"
"None but self," cried Buck, "to
    blame!
Mischief is not life's true aim!"
Then said gravely Teacher Lämpel,
"There again is an example!"
"To be sure! bad thing for youth,"
Said the Baker, "a sweet tooth!"
Even Uncle says, "Good folks!
See what comes of stupid jokes!"
But the honest farmer: "Guy!
What concern is that to I?"
Through the place in short there
    went
One wide murmur of content:
"God be praised! the town is free
From this great rascality!"

Als man dies im Dorf erfuhr,
War von Trauer keine Spur.
Witwe Bolte, mild und weich,
Sprach: ,,Sieh da, ich dacht es
    gleich!"
,,Ja, ja, ja!" rief Meister Böck,
,,Bosheit ist kein Lebenszweck!"
Drauf so sprach Herr Lehrer
    Lämpel:
,,Dies ist wieder ein Exempel!"
,,Freilich!" meint' der Zuckerbäcker,
,,Warum ist der Mensch so
    lecker?!"
Selbst der gute Onkel Fritze
Sprach: ,,Das kommt von dumme
    Witze!"
Doch der brave Bauersmann
Dachte: ,,Wat geiht meck dat
    an?!"
Kurz, im ganzen Ort herum
Ging ein freudiges Gebrumm:
,,Gott sei Dank! Nun ist's vorbei
Mit der Übeltäterei!!"

II

KER AND PLUNK

Two Dogs and Two Boys

(Plisch und Plum)

Translated, freely, by H. Arthur Klein and M. C. Klein

A pipe is jutting from his face;
His arms hold two young dogs in
  place.

This is old man Kaspar Schlee;
He can smoke quite fearfully.
Yet, though his pipe is burning hot,
His heart's not warm—distinctly
  not!

Eine Pfeife in dem Munde,
Unterm Arm zwei junge Hunde

Trug der alte Kaspar Schlich. –
Rauchen kann er fürchterlich.
Doch, obschon die Pfeife glüht,
Oh, wie kalt ist sein Gemüt! –

"What good," he asks, rhetorically,
"Would be two dogs like these to
  me?

Would they perhaps provide me
  fun?
My answer's 'No!'—for two, or one.
When I don't like a thing, I got to
Toss it out! Yes, that's my motto!"

,,Wozu" – lauten seine Worte –
,,Wozu nützt mir diese Sorte?

Macht sie mir vielleicht Pläsier?
Einfach nein! erwidr' ich mir.
Wenn mir aber was nicht lieb,
Weg damit! ist mein Prinzip."

Ker and Plunk

At the pond he halts and pauses,
For there he means to drown the
   dogses.

An dem Teiche steht er still,
Weil er sie ertränken will.

Both frightened quadrupeds are
   pawing,
And the air they're wildly clawing;
For an inner voice has told 'em
Not to trust the man who holds 'em.

Ängstlich strampeln beide kleinen
Quadrupeden mit den Beinen;
Denn die innre Stimme spricht;
Der Geschichte trau ich nicht! –

Allay! And through the air one flies.

Hubs! fliegt einer schon im Bogen.

Oops! And in the pond he lies.

Plisch! da glitscht er in die Wogen.

Holah! The second doggie follows.   Hubs! der zweite hinterher.

Ker-plunk! He, too, in water
wallows.   Plum!! damit verschwindet er.

"That's that!" cries Schlee; he
  puffs, and then
He goes off on his way again.
But here—in fact, to every man—
Events don't work out as per plan.

,,Abgemacht!" rief Kaspar Schlich,
Dampfte und entfernte sich.
Aber hier, wie überhaupt,
Kommt es anders, als man glaubt.

Plisch und Plum

Here are Paul and Peter coming—
(They've just undressed to do some
  swimming
And from their hideout they could
  scan
The carrying-out of Kaspar's plan.)

Paul und Peter, welche grade
Sich entblößt zu einem Bade,
Gaben stillverborgen acht,
Was der böse Schlich gemacht.

Now, quickly, like a pair of frogs,
They're diving in to save those
  dogs.

Hurtig und den Fröschen gleich
Hupfen beide in den Teich.

And each boy, with a helping hand,
Ferries a puppy safe to land.

Jeder bringt in seiner Hand
Einen kleinen Hund ans Land.

Ker and Plunk

"*Ker!*" cries Paul, "I'm naming mine!"
"*Plunk!*" says Peter, "will fit mine fine!"

„Plisch" – rief Paul – „so nenn ich meinen."
Plum – so nannte Peter seinen.

And so, now Paul and Pete march home,
Each with his puppy in his arm.
They hurry, but they still take care
To bring their doggies safely there.

Und so tragen Paul und Peter
Ihre beiden kleinen Köter
Eilig, doch mit aller Schonung,
Hin zur elterlichen Wohnung.

CHAPTER TWO

Papa Field is honest, true—
Mama Field is loving, too.
Arm in arm they sit, as one,

Papa Fittig, treu und friedlich,
Mama Fittig, sehr gemütlich,
Sitzen, Arm in Arm geschmiegt,

Together, in the setting sun.
They both enjoy the peace they
    feel;
For soon will come the evening
    meal,
And, to round out a lovely day,
Their boys are now due home from
    play.

Sorgenlos und stillvergnügt
Kurz vor ihrem Abendschmause
Noch ein wenig vor dem Hause,
Denn der Tag war ein gelinder,
Und erwarten ihre Kinder.

Plisch und Plum

See, here—both boys have come in view—	Sieh, da kommen alle zwei,
And Ker and Plunk are with them, too.	Plisch und Plum sind auch dabei. –
This doesn't look so good to Dad.	Dies scheint aber nichts für Fittig.

In fact, he's starting to get mad.	Heftig ruft er: „Na, da bitt ich!"
But Mama in her winning way	Doch Mama mit sanften Mienen:
Says, "Now, then, Daddy—it's okay!"	„Fittig!!" – bat sie – „gönn' es ihnen!!"

Then, because their supper's
   waiting,
They enter, without hesitating.

Angerichtet stand die frische
Abendmilch schon auf dem Tische.

But as they do—of course, we
   knew it—
There's Ker and Plunk who beat
   them to it!

Freudig eilen sie ins Haus;
Plisch und Plum geschwind voraus.

Oh, dear! It's like some dreadful
   dream;
Both dogs are now paw-deep in
   cream!
Their pleasure's noisy—while
they're lapping,
Their tongues make a melodious
   slapping.

Ach, da stehn sie ohne Scham
Mitten in dem süßen Rahm
Und bekunden ihr Behagen
Durch ein lautes Zungenschlagen.

69

Ker and Plunk

Schlee, who through the window's
gawking,
Cries in surprise: "It's really
shocking!

Schlich, der durch das Fenster sah,
Ruft verwundert: „Ei, sieh da!

A nuisance, this—admittedly,
Tee-hee, tee-hee!—But not for *me!*"

Das ist freilich ärgerlich,
Hehe! aber nicht für mich!!"

As if that fuss had never been,
Now Paul and Peter here are seen.
They're resting in their little beds.
Why should they trouble their
  small heads?
They sleep in peace, while through
  each nose
A gentle snoring softly goes.

Paul und Peter, ungerührt,
Grad als wäre nichts passiert,
Ruhn in ihrem Schlafgemach;
Denn was fragen sie darnach.
Ein uns aus durch ihre Nasen
Säuselt ein gelindes Blasen.

However, Ker and Plunk as yet   Plisch und Plum hingegen scheinen

Ker and Plunk

Don't seem to be completely set   **Noch nicht recht mit sich im reinen**

On where to pick a place to rest—   **In betreff der Lagerstätte.**

But, bed's the answer to their quest.   **Schließlich gehn sie auch zu Bette.**

Plisch und Plum

Now Ker, as if still on the ground,
Turns himself slowly three times
  round,

Unser Plisch, gewohnterweise,
Dreht sich dreimal erst im Kreise.

While Plunk takes his dear master's
  face
And holds it in a fond embrace.

Unser Plum dagegen zeigt
Sich zur Zärtlichkeit geneigt.

But boys who like to sleep at night
Don't find such goings-on quite
  right.

Denen, die der Ruhe pflegen,
Kommen manche ungelegen.

Ker and Plunk

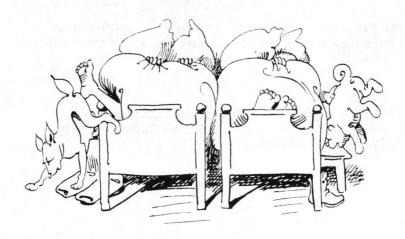

"Scram!"—When *that* harsh word's been said
Both dogs are pitched clear out of bed.

Now cool air stirs them both to action,
And action serves as a distraction.

„Marsch!" – Mit diesem barschen Wort
Stößt man sie nach außen fort. –

Kühle weckt die Tätigkeit;
Tätigkeit verkürzt die Zeit.

And very welcome, to their mind,
Are both the pants and shoe they find,
Which, before the next day's dawn—

Sehr willkommen sind dazu
Hier die Hose, da der Schuh;
Welche, eh der Tag beginnt,

Plisch und Plum

Fantastic forms have taken on.	Auch bereits verändert sind.
To dear Dad, it looks quite bad When he comes in to wake each lad.	Für den Vater, welch ein Schrecken, Als er kam und wollte wecken.

| Indeed, his heart is tempest-tossed. He asks, "How much will all this cost?" | Der Gedanke macht ihn blaß, Wenn er fragt: Was kostet das? |

He would vent spankings without
   number
Upon his sons, who still feign
   slumber.

Schon will er die Knaben strafen,
Welche tun, als ob sie schlafen.

But Mama pleads again, "Dear
   Dad,
Please don't make our boys sad!"
And these fair words, so full of
   love,
Really cool poor Papa off . . .

Doch die Mutter fleht: ,,Ich bitt
   dich,
Sei nicht grausam, bester Fittig!!"
Diese Worte liebevoll
Schmelzen seinen Vatergroll.

Plisch und Plum

It's all the same to Pete and Paul
If they have no good clothes at all.
Pete wears big slippers on his feet;
Paul's trousers—well, they don't
   look *neat!*

Paul und Peter ist's egal.
Peter geht vorerst einmal
In zwei Schlapp-Pantoffeln los,
Paul in seiner Zackenhos'.

And dogs who don't know how to
   act
Into the doghouse must be packed!

Plisch und Plum, weil ohne Sitte,
Kommen in die Hundehütte.

Ker and Plunk

Now Schlee observes, "Cruel
    destiny!
Tee-hee!—But really not for me!"

„Ist fatal!" – bemerkte Schlich –
„Hehe! aber nicht für mich!"

CHAPTER FOUR

VIERTES KAPITEL

At last inside this cage confined—
A mouse—the freshest of his kind.

Endlich fing im Drahtgehäuse
Sich die frechste aller Mäuse,

He'd turned the household inside
    out
Whenever Mamma was about;
And, worst of all, in dead of night
Had given her many an awful
    fright.

Welche Mama Fittig immer,
Bald im Keller, bald im Zimmer,
Und besonders bei der Nacht,
Fürchterlich nervös gemacht.

Plisch und Plum

This mouse, they think, would be
  quite nice
To give to Ker and Plunk as prize,
So now they say, "Get out! *Heraus!*
You nasty, evil, nibbling mouse!"

Ooops! The mouse, in search of
  safety,

Dieses gibt für Plisch und Plum
Ein erwünschtes Gaudium;
Denn jetzt heißt es: ,,Mal heraus,
Alte, böse Knuspermaus!"

Husch! des Peters Hosenbein,

Up Peter's pant-leg dashes, hasty.

Denkt sie, soll ihr Schutz verleihn.

Ker and Plunk

Ker follows after with his snout;
Plunk waits for mousie to pop out.

Plisch verfolgt sie in das Rohr;
Plum steht anderseits davor.

Click! Mousie's teeth are nipping
  where
Plunk sniffs and breathes the
  ambient air.

Knipp! in sein Geruchsorgan
Bohrt die Maus den Nagezahn.

Plisch und Plum

Ker seeks to give this tail an
ending,

Plisch will sie am Schwanze ziehn,

But look how mousie is defending!   Knipp! am Ohre hat sie ihn.

Ker and Plunk

And now, you see, the mouse has fled	Siehst du wohl, da läuft sie hin
Into the neighbor's tulip-bed.	In das Beet der Nachbarin.
Dig in, dig out! Oh, double woe,	Kritzekratze, wehe dir,
As dearest flowers in fragments go!	Du geliebte Blumenzier!

Plisch und Plum

Madam Kimmel here is seen
Filling her lamp with kerosene.
At her garden now she glances—
Her heart with horror writhes and
    dances!

Madam Kümmel will soeben
Öl auf ihre Lampe geben.
Fast wär ihr das Herz geknickt,
Als sie in den Garten blickt.

She fairly flies out to the scene,
Clutching the can of kerosene.

Sie beflügelt ihren Schritt,
Und die Kanne bringt sie mit.

Ker and Plunk

Furious, but with sadistic pleasure,	Zornig, aber mit Genuß
She pours upon each dog a	Gibt sie jedem einen Guß;
measure;	Erst dem Plisch und dann dem
One pour for Plunk and one for	Plum.
Ker.	Scharf ist das Petroleum;
The kerosene stings skin and fur.	

It produces "side-effects"	Und die Wirkung, die es macht,
Exceeding all that she expects!	Hat Frau Kümmel nicht bedacht.

But now each suffering doggie's
  antic
Drives Madam Kimmel nearly
  frantic;
So, as her madlike state begins,
She closes both her eyes and
  grins. . . .

Aber was sich nun begibt,
Macht Frau Kümmel so betrübt,
Daß sie, wie von Wahn umfächelt,
Ihre Augen schließt und lächelt.

Sighing, "O-o-o-o!" so sad and
    quaint,
She falls down in a total faint.

Mit dem Seufzerhauche: U!
Stößt ihr eine Ohnmacht zu.

Plisch und Plum

Cold and callous, Pete and Paul
Show no sympathy at all;
Strangers' painful psychic smarts
Fail to stir their saucy hearts.

Paul und Peter, frech und kühl,
Zeigen wenig Mitgefühl;
Fremder Leute Seelenschmerzen
Nehmen sie sich nicht zu Herzen.

Now Schlee observes, "Cruel
  destiny!—
Tee-hee!—But really not for me..."

„Ist fatal!" – bemerkte Schlich –
„Hehe! aber nicht für mich."

Ker and Plunk, it's all too clear,
Are a miserable pair;
Dog-delinquents, but as one,
And when all is said and done,
Each an admirable creature.
But—how long? And can you
    feature
Rascal One plus Rascal Two?—
In the long run, it won't do!

Plisch und Plum, wie leider klar,
Sind ein niederträchtig Paar;
Niederträchtig, aber einig,
Und in letzter Hinsicht, mein ich,
Immerhin noch zu verehren;
Doch wie lange wird es währen?
Bösewicht mit Bösewicht
Auf die Dauer geht es nicht.

* Chapter Five is not included here.

Here a-basking in the sun	Vis-à-vis im Sonnenschein
A little dog—a pretty one!	Saß ein Hündchen hübsch und klein,
Great joy now grows within these two	Dieser Anblick ist für beide
Through this unexpected view.	Eine unverhoffte Freude.

Ker and Plunk

Each would like to stand as first To gaze at her for whom they thirst.	Jeder möchte vorne stehen, Um entzückt hinauf zu spähen.
If Ker pushes to the fore, Then Plunk starts feeling mighty sore.	Hat sich Plisch hervorgedrängt, Fühlt der Plum sich tief gekränkt.

But if Plunk assumes first place, Ker makes a real disgusted face.	Drängt nach vorne sich der Plum, Nimmt der Plisch die Sache krumm.

Plisch und Plum

Already there's a warning growling;
Then footwork starts, and eyes are
    rolling!

Schon erhebt sich dumpfes Grollen,
Füße scharren, Augen rollen,

A heated battle's now beginning;

Und der heiße Kampf beginnt;

Plunk must run, for Ker is winning.

Plum muß laufen, Plisch gewinnt.

Ker and Plunk

In the kitchen, Mama makes
Salad and her good pancakes—
Dishes that mean special joys
To both her hungry, watching
boys.

Mama Fittig machte grad
Pfannenkuchen und Salat,
Das bekannte Leibgericht,
Was so sehr zum Herzen spricht.

Hey! Here's Plunk, that dog-
    disaster;
Behind him, Ker is following faster.

Hurr! da kommt mit Ungestüm
Plum, und Plisch ist hinter ihm.

Stool and pot and batter fall;	Schemel, Topf und Kuchenbrei
Confusion triumphs over all!	Mischt sich in die Beißerei. –
"Just you wait, Ker!" Pete lets	„Warte, Plisch! du Schwerenöter!"
fly—	Damit reichte ihm der Peter
A blow that strikes a real bull's	Einen wohlgezielten Hieb.
eye.	Das ist aber Paul nicht lieb.
But this blow angers watching Paul.	

Plisch und Plum

"You shouldn't have hit my dog at all!"
And Paul whips Peter on the ankle,
A blow that's really bound to rankle.

„Warum schlägst du meinen Köter?"
Ruft der Paul und haut den Peter.

Peter isn't paralyzed;
He lashes Paul about the eyes.

Dieser auch nicht angefroren,
Klatscht dem Paul um seine Ohren.

Ker and Plunk

Now they're at it, hot and hasty.
Oh, that salad dish, so tasty!
It's serving each embattled brother
To besmear and mess the other!

Jetzt wird's aber desperat. –
Ach, der köstliche Salat
Dient den aufgeregten Geistern,
Sich damit zu überkleistern.

Plisch und Plum

Papa rapidly draws near
With his stick upraised in air.
Mama, full of mildness still,
Seeks to mitigate this ill.
"Dearest Papa," she implores,
"Control yourself just this once
     more."
Great for a mate to arbitrate!
But, wait—see more of Mama's
     fate—.

Papa Fittig kommt gesprungen
Mit dem Stocke hochgeschwungen.
Mama Fittig, voller Güte,
Daß sie dies Malheur verhüte:
,,Bester Fittig" – ruft sie – ,,faß
     dich!"
Dabei ist sie etwas hastig.

Ker and Plunk

Mama's bonnet, fine and new,
Is catastrophically run through.
"Tee-hee!" Schlee with malice
  chuckles,
"As I see, they have their
  troubles!"

Ihre Haube, zart umflort,
Wird von Fittigs Stock durchbohrt.
,,Hehe!" – lacht der böse
  Schlich –
,,Wie ich sehe, hat man sich!"

Plisch und Plum

Who gloats while others woe endure
Is mostly quite disliked—that's sure!

Wer sich freut, wenn wer betrübt,
Macht sich meistens unbeliebt.

This pancake-hat, with Schlee connected,
Is mighty hot and unexpected.

Lästig durch die große Hitze
Ist die Pfannenkuchenmütze.

"Most deadly!" here remarks Herr Schlee.
"But—this time it touches *me!*"

„Höchst fatal!" – bemerkte Schlich –
„Aber diesmal auch für mich!"

Here Ker and Plunk are full of
  grief;
They whine and howl without
  relief.
For, see, two tight, confining
  chains
Have got them under close
  constraint.

Seht, da sitzen Plisch und Plum
Voll Verdruß und machen brumm!
Denn zwei Ketten, gar nicht lang,
Hemmen ihren Tatendrang.

And Papa has begun to falter.
"This"—he thinks—"has got to
  alter!
Virtue needs a helping hand;
Evil can make a solo stand!"

Und auch Fittig hat Beschwerden.
,,Dies" – denkt er – ,,muß anders
  werden!
Tugend will ermuntert sein,
Bosheit kann man schon allein!"

Therefore, we here see Paul and
  Peter
Before Herr Bockelman, the
  teacher.
And learned Master Bockelman
Begins in this way to go on:

Daher sitzen Paul und Peter
Jetzt vor Bokelmanns Katheder;
Und Magister Bokelmann
Hub, wie folgt, zu reden an:

"My dear boys, it's a joy to see
That you have come hither to learn
  from me,
And—as I trust—with all your
  power,
To watch and listen every hour.
Now, first:—Let's be industrious to
  heed
How to write, to reckon, and to
  read,
Recalling that men through skills
  of such sort
Gain bread and meat and good
  report.

,,Geliebte Knaben, ich bin erfreut,
Daß ihr nunmehro gekommen seid,
Um, wie ich hoffe, mit allen
  Kräften
Augen und Ohren auf mich zu
  heften. –
Zum ersten: Lasset uns fleißig
  betreiben
Lesen, Kopf-, Tafelrechnen und
  Schreiben,
Alldieweil der Mensch durch sotane
  Künste
Zu Ehren gelanget und
  Brotgewinste.

Second: How far with all that
  would we get
If we lacked a courteous etiquette?
For he who is not at all times
  polite
Will have trouble and grief on
  every side.
Therefore, in conclusion—for this
  is my way—
I beg you sincerely—in fact, I
  pray—

Zum zweiten: Was würde das aber
  besagen
Ohne ein höfliches Wohlbetragen;
Denn wer nicht höflich nach allen
  Seiten,
Hat doch nur lauter
  Verdrießlichkeiten,
Darum zum Schlusse, – denn
  sehet, so bin ich –
Bitt ich euch dringend, inständigst
  und innig,

If you each have decided, deep
  down in your heart
To follow my teaching and all I
  impart,
Then give me your hand, and when
  I am done,
Look at me and say: 'Yes, indeed,
  Herr Bockelman!'"

Habt ihr beschlossen in eurem
  Gemüte,
Meiner Lehre zu folgen in aller
  Güte,
So reichet die Hände und blicket
  mich an
Und sprechet: Jawohl, Herr
  Bokelmann!"

Paul and Peter are thinking with
  joy:
"Is that how it is with this
  silly old boy?"
They speak not a single word in
  reply
But sit there and giggle, "Hee-hee!"
  and "Hi-hi!"
Then Bockelman, who has whistled
  while waiting,
Speaks up once again without
  hesitating:

Paul und Peter denken froh:
„Alter Junge, bist du so??"
Keine Antwort geben sie,
Sondern machen bloß hihi!
Worauf er, der leise pfiff,
Wiederum das Wort ergriff.

"Since you're each of a mind to
   harden your heart
And continue rascality—hear what
   I impart:
I, for my part, do not feel I should
   back turn
Until I have placed you face down
   on my lectern.
In this way, and without taking it
   under advisement,
I'll proceed, by the means of some
   healthy chastisement,
To soften the both of your
   hardened young spirits . . ."

,,Dieweil ihr denn gesonnen" –
   so spricht er –
,,Euch zu verhärten als
   Bösewichter,
So bin ich gesonnen, euch
   dahingegen
Allhier mal über das Pult zu legen,
Um solchermaßen mit einigen
   Streichen
Die harten Gemüter euch zu
   erweichen."

So saying, he takes from his
   jacket, or near it,

Flugs hervor aus seinem Kleide,
Wie den Säbel aus der Scheide,

105

Ker and Plunk

A hazel-root stick, like a sword
  from its case;
And, reaching around to the back
  of each face,
With a well practised hand he
  grabs the stout collars
Of both of these young and
  intransigeant scholars.

Zieht er seine harte, gute,
Schlanke, schwanke Haselrute,
Faßt mit kund'ger Hand im Nacken
Paul und Peter bei den Jacken

With them thus united he lays it
  on—
Until he thinks that the job's been
  well done.

Und verklopft sie so vereint,
Bis es ihm genügend scheint.

"Now, then,"—in a tone that's
    calm and ample—
"What do you say, my dear boys,
    to that sample?

„Nunmehr" – so sprach er in
    guter Ruh –
„Meine lieben Knaben, was sagt ihr
    dazu??

Are you now contented?—And are
    we agreed?"
"Oh, yes, Herr Bockelman! Yes,
    indeed!!"

Seid ihr zufrieden und sind wir
    einig??"
„Jawohl, Herr Bokelmann!" riefen
    sie schleunig.

Ker and Plunk

So Bockelman's method, as we see,	Dies ist Bokelmanns Manier.
Succeeded, oh, quite famously;	Daß sie gut, das sehen wir.
And everyone who has an eyeful	Jeder sagte, jeder fand:

Finds, "Paul and Peter are
   delightful!"
And for Ker and Plunk, to boot,
Come lessons with the hazel-
   root. . .
Just as applied by Bockelman.
So, then, when their new
   schooling's done,

„Paul und Peter sind scharmant!!"
Aber auch für Plisch und Plum
Nahte sich das Studium
Und die nötige Dressur,
Ganz wie Bokelmann verfuhr.

Both dogs are truly highly trained,
And popular, because restrained.

Bald sind beide kunstgeübt,
Daher allgemein beliebt,

And, next—as properly takes
    place—
Profit runs Art a real close race.

Und, wie das mit Recht geschieht,
Auf die Kunst folgt der Profit.

Conclusion

Travelling in this neighborhood,
A chap whose wealth is more than
   good—
In his hand, a telescope,
Comes this Mister, known as
   "Hope."
"Why not,"—and here it's Hope
   who's talking—
"Watch distant things, the while
   I'm walking?
It's lovely *there*, as like as not,
And I am *here*, no matter what!"

Zugereist in diese Gegend,
Noch viel mehr als sehr vermögend,
In der Hand das Perspektiv,
Kam ein Mister namens Pief.
„Warum soll ich nicht beim
   Gehen" –
Sprach er – „in die Ferne sehen?
Schön ist es auch anderswo,
Und hier bin ich sowieso."

110

Plisch und Plum

And, saying so, he somehow
  stumbles
And straight into the pond he
  tumbles.

Hierbei aber stolpert er
In den Teich und sieht nichts mehr.

"My dear boys Paul and Peter,
  say,
Where *is* that Mister, anyway?"

„Paul und Peter, meine Lieben,
Wo ist denn der Herr geblieben?"

So asks Herr Field, who here is
  seen
Strolling for pleasure where it's
  green.

Fragte Fittig, der mit ihnen
Hier spazieren geht im Grünen.

Ker and Plunk

But Papa scarce need ask his
    dears;
The Mister presently appears—

Doch wo der geblieben war,
Wird ihm ohne dieses klar.

Minus telescope and hat,
Hope emerges, just like that . . .

Ohne Perspektiv und Hut
Steigt er ruhig aus der Flut.

"Go fetch, now—Ker and Plunk—
    to hand!"
So sounds out the boys' command.

„Allez, Plisch und Plum, apport!"
Tönte das Kommandowort.

Plisch und Plum

Well trained to fetch and carry too,
The dogs dive, and are lost to view,
But they'll succeed, you must
believe;
They're quite accustomed to
retrieve.
See—Plunk brings back the
telescope,
And Ker—the hat of Mister Hope.
Now Hope remarks, "It's clear—
oh, quite!—
These dogs are bits of old all right!

Streng gewöhnt an das Parieren,
Tauchen sie und apportieren
Das Vermißte prompt und schnell.
Mister Pief sprach: „Weriwell!
Diese zwei gefallen mir!

One hundred marks I'm offering
you."
Says Papa quickly: "That will
do!"

Wollt ihr hundert Mark dafür?"
Drauf erwidert Papa Fittig
Ohne weiters: „Ei, da bitt ich."

Ker and Plunk

Pop feels as if he's made anew,
When so much money meets his
view.

Er fühlt sich wie neugestärkt,
Als er soviel Geld bemerkt.

"Now then, Ker and Plunk, you
   two—
Keep well, for we must say adieu.
Oh, just to think—it was right here,
And the time is just a year,
Since that moment, bitter-sweet,
When all four of us did meet.
Yes, 'twas just one year ago
When we formed our foursome!—
   So
Live happily and free from need,
And on best British beefsteak
   feed!"

„Also, Plisch und Plum, ihr beiden,
Lebet wohl, wir müssen scheiden,
Ach, an dieser Stelle hier,
Wo vor einem Jahr wir vier
In so schmerzlich süßer Stunde
Uns vereint zum schönen Bunde;
Lebt vergnügt und ohne Not,
Beefsteak sei euer täglich Brot!"

Schlee's come by, too, to spy a
  trifle.
And now he's *really* got an eyeful!
Good luck for others he can't bear;
It hits him hard, right then and
  there.
"Most gratifying," murmurs he,
"But not for *me*, unfortunately!"

Schlich, der auch herbeigekommen,
Hat dies alles wahrgenommen.
Fremdes Glück ist ihm zu schwer.
„Recht erfreulich!" murmelt er –
„Aber leider nicht für mich!!"

Suddenly, he feels a spasm
As envy grips his heart and has
  him.
(Covetousness, inward working,
Has set his psycho-soma jerking!)
He puffs some smoke, and then—
  he misses—

Plötzlich fühlt er einen Stich,
Kriegt vor Neid den Seelenkrampf,
Macht geschwind noch etwas
  Dampf,

Falls in the water, so it hisses.   Fällt ins Wasser, daß es zischt,

Thus the brief candle that was Schlee   Und der Lebensdocht erlischt.
Is now extinguished, utterly.

Once animated by his breath,   Einst belebt von seinem Hauche,
And now when he is felled by   Jetzt mit spärlich mattem Rauche
　death,   Glimmt die Pfeife noch so weiter
His pipe still smolders on, indeed   Und verzehrt die letzten Kräuter.
Consuming the remaining weed.   Noch ein Wölkchen blau und
One wisp of smoke—a curly one—   　kraus –
Then, phfffft!—the story is all   Phütt! ist die Geschichte

done.

Miscellaneous Mischief-makers:

More or Less Human

III

THE EGGHEAD AND THE TWO CUT-UPS OF CORINTH
(Diogenes und die bösen Buben von Korinth)
Translated, freely, by H. Arthur Klein and M. C. Klein

Here's the famed Diogenes—
Seen, at least, below his knees—
His barrel turned to catch the sun,
Lies the meditating one.

Nachdenklich liegt in seiner Tonne
Diogenes hier an der Sonne.

A kid who sees the wise man's feet,
Summons his friend; they'll have a
  treat!

Ein Bube, der ihn liegen sah,
Ruft seinen Freund; gleich ist er da.

The Egghead and the Two Cut-ups

And now the saucy little jerks
Knock hard, to give the sage the
works.

Nun fangen die zwei Tropfen
Am Fasse an zu klopfen.

Diogenes is looking out.
"Hey! What's doing!?" is his
shout.

Diogenes schaut aus dem Faß
Und spricht: „Ei, ei, was soll denn
das!?"

Diogenes und die bösen Buben

The youngster with the Grecian hat Brings up his squirt gun, just for that.	Der Bube mit der Mütze Holt seine Wasserspritze.

The gun's expertly pumped and poked; Diogenes is simply soaked.	Er spritzt durchs Spundloch in das Faß. Diogenes wird pudelnaß.

The Egghead and the Two Cut-ups

He's hardly laid him down again	Kaum legt Diogenes sich nieder,
Before the naughty little men	So kommen die bösen Buben wieder.

Go at the barrel with great shoves.	Sie gehn ans Faß und schieben es;
"Stop!" yells the wise man, as it moves.	„Halt, halt!" schreit da Diogenes.

Diogenes und die bösen Buben

The good man gets all dizzy;
He's really in a tizzy.

Ganz schwindlich wird der Brave. –
Paßt auf! Jetzt kommt die Strafe.

The boys now note with panicked
    looks—
This barrel has two nails, like
    hooks.

Zwei Nägel, die am Fasse stecken,
Fassen die Buben bei den Röcken.

The Egghead and the Two Cut-ups

They kick and shriek and cry.
In vain, escape they try.

Die bösen Buben weinen
Und zappeln mit den Beinen.

All shred of hope is gone;
The barrel's rolling on.

Da hilft kein Weinen und kein
Schrei'n,
Sie müssen unter's Faß hinein.

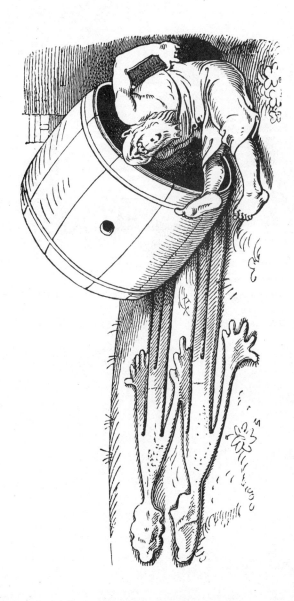

Now Corinth's cut-ups, head to toe,
Are rolled out flat, like cookie
dough.

Die bösen Buben von Korinth
Sind platt gewalzt, wie Kuchen
sind.

The Egghead and the Two Cut-ups

The sage crawls back into his
 barrel.
"This leads to that!" is his wise
 moral.

Diogenes der Weise aber kroch ins
 Faß
Und sprach: ,,Ja, ja, das kommt
 von das!!"

IV

THE RAVEN-ROBBIN' RASCALS

(*Das Rabennest*)

Translated, freely, by H. Arthur Klein

Two little rascals, young and gay,   Zwei Knaben, jung und heiter,
Ladder-equipped, are under way.   Die tragen eine Leiter.

The nest has three young ravens in it;
"We'll have those birdies in a minute."

Im Nest die jungen Raben,
Die werden wir gleich haben.

Das Rabennest

The ladder's fallen instantly;
The ravens look on cheerfully.

Da fällt die Leiter um im Nu,
Die Raben sehen munter zu.

The three now cry out, chorally, "Their legs are all that one can see!"	Sie schreien im Vereine, Man sieht nur noch die Beine!

Das Rabennest

| The hunter comes up with dispatch, | Der Jäger kommt an diesen Ort |
| He gives command, "Go, Fido, fetch!" | Und spricht zu seinem Hund: „Apport!" |

| The dog retrieves one soaking boy; | Den Knaben apportiert der Hund, |
| The hunter smokes his pipe with joy. | Der Jäger hat die Pfeif' im Mund. |

133

"Now, fetch to me that other one!"   „Nun hole auch den andern her!"
The dog, however, is all done. . . .   Der Schlingel aber will nicht mehr.

The hunter is obliged to jump   Der Jäger muß sich selbst bemühn,
And pull the other from the swamp.   Den Knaben aus dem Sumpf zu
                      ziehn.

| Both boys go slowly trudging back; | Zur Hälfte sind die Knaben |
| One half of each is raven-black. | So schwarz als wie die Raben. |

| This dog won't fetch, nor hunter shoot, | Der Hund und auch der Jägersmann, |
| So black are they on paw and boot. | Die haben schwarze Stiefel an. |

But high up, in the raven nest,
The ravens' joy is well expressed.

Die Raben in dem Rabennest
Sind aber kreuzfidel gewest.

V

DECEITFUL HENRY

(*Der hinterlistige Heinrich*)

Translated, freely, by H. Arthur Klein and M. C. Klein

The mother says, "Oh, Henry, do
Receive this pretzel; it's for you."

Die Mutter sprach: „O Heinrich
    mein!
Nimm diese Brezen, sie sei dein!"

But naughty Henry reckons quick
"Now I'll catch geese here with
    this trick."

Der böse Heinrich denkt sich
    gleich:
„Jetzt fang' ich Gänse auf dem
    Teich."

Deceitful Henry

A gosling's swimming toward the land.
Snap!—Henry grabs it in his hand.

Ein junges Gänslein schwamm ans Land;
Schwapp! hat es Heinrich in der Hand.

It cries and struggles fearfully;
Its parents are in agony.

Es schreit und zappelt fürchterlich;
Die Alten sind ganz außer sich.

Der hinterlistige Heinrich

The goose, with one tremendous bite,
Now holds the pants of Henry tight.

Jetzt faßt die Gans den Heinrich an,
Wo sie zunächst ihn fassen kann.

Here Henry's fallen on his rear.
A goose is nipping at each ear.

Der Heinrich fällt auf seinen Rücken;
Am Ohr tun ihn die Gänse zwicken.

Deceitful Henry

They're flying now—Oh, have a care!—
With Henry, high into the air.

Sie fliegen dann, o weh, o weh!
Mit Heinrich fort und in die Höh'.

Now just above his chimney tall
The geese have let bad Henry fall.

Hoch über seiner Mutter Haus
Da lassen sie den Heinrich aus.

Der hinterlistige Heinrich

He drops all black, a falling blot,
Right into Mother's boiling pot.

Der fällt ganz schwarz und über
  Kopf
Der Mutter in den Suppentopf.

With fork and strength, with bend
  and stoop,
His mother hauls him from the
  soup.

Mit einer Gabel und mit Müh'
Zieht ihn die Mutter aus der Brüh'.

Deceitful Henry

Here Henry, drying, looks a sight—
It serves the little rascal right!

Hier sieht man ihn am Ofen
    stehn—
Dem Schlingel ist ganz recht
    geschehn!

The geese, however, pleased as
    punch,
Eat Henry's pretzel for their lunch.

Die Gänse aber voll Ergötzen
Verzehren Heinrichs braune
    Brezen.

VI

THE BOY AND THE POPGUN

The Story of Naughty Frank and His Terrible Popgun
(*Das Pusterohr*)

Translated by Abby Langdon Alger

Here sits old Bartelmann a' sipping
His tea, in which a crust he's
   dipping.

Hier sitzt Herr Bartelmann im
   Frei'n
Und taucht sich eine Brezel ein.

Frank with his popgun standing
   near
Hits Bartelmann upon the ear.

Der Franz mit seinem Pusterohr
Schießt Bartelmann ans linke Ohr.

| Good gracious me, so thinketh he, | „Ei, Zapperment" – so denkt sich der – |
| From under here it sure must be. | „Das kam ja wohl von unten her!" |

| Oh no, thinks he, this cannot be | „Doch nein" – denkt er – „es kann nicht sein!" |
| And dips his pretzel in his tea. | Und taucht die Brezel wieder ein. |

Das Pusterohr

Pop—from his hand the crust is flying,
Old Bartelmann of fright's near dying.

Und – witsch – getroffen ist die Brezen,
Herrn Bartelmann erfaßt Entsetzen.

Then at his eye Frank aimed a dart;
Which made it sorely ache and smart.

Und – witsch – jetzt trifft die Kugel gar
Das Aug', das sehr empfindlich war.

The Boy and the Popgun

So that the tears all swiftly ran
Down cheeks of old Bartelmann.

So daß dem braven Bartelmann
Die Träne aus dem Auge rann.

Good gracious me, so thinketh he—
From up above, it sure must be!

„Ei, Zapperment" – so denkt sich
der –
„Das kommt ja wohl von oben
her!" –

Das Pusterohr

Oh ho! he falls—for hurry scurry
Frank hits his nose in greatest
    flurry.

Aujau! Er fällt – denn mit Geblase
Schießt Franz den Pfeil ihm in die
    Nase.

See now he sparkles at the thought;
Behind the fence the rascal's
    caught.

Da denkt Herr Bartelmann: „Aha!
Dies spitze Ding, das kenn' ich ja!"

The Boy and the Popgun

When Bartelmann the dart espies,
An old acquaintance greets his eyes.

Und freudig kommt ihm der
    Gedanke:
Der Franz steht hinter dieser
    Planke!

With coffee-pot he now doth gloat
To drive the popgun down Frank's
    throat!

Und – klapp! schlägt er mit
    seinem Topf
Das Pusterohr tief in den Kopf!

148

Das Pusterohr

Take warning hence, you naughty
  chicks,
On older folks play no more tricks!

Drum schieß mit deinem Püstericht
Auf keine alten Leute nicht!

VII

ICE-PETER

The Story of the Foolish Boy Who Would Go Skating

(Der Eispeter:
Eine Bilderposse)

Translated by Abby Langdon Alger

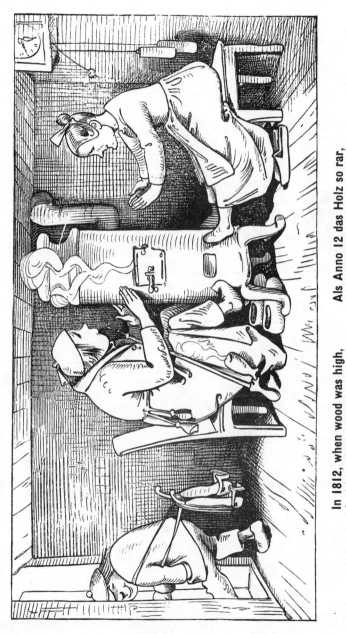

In 1812, when wood was high,
And icy winter all did try;

Most stayed at home a-toasting,
But Peter would go skating,
coasting.

Als Anno 12 das Holz so rar,
Und als der kalte Winter war,

Da blieb ein jeder gern zu Haus;
Nur Peter muß aufs Eis hinaus.

It was so cold outside, they said,
That from the branches, birds fell
dead.

Old Uncle Forster begged and
warned him
To keep in-doors, but Peter
scorned him.

Da draußen, ja, man glaubt es
kaum,
Fiel manche Krähe tot vom Baum.

Der Onkel Förster warnt und
spricht:
,,Mein Peter, heute geht es nicht!"

Der Eispeter

A little rabbit too was found,
Quite stiff, fast frozen to the
ground.

Still Peter sings in merry tone
And takes his seat upon a stone.

Auch ist ein Hase bei den Ohren
Ganz dicht am Wege festgefroren.

Doch Peter denkt: Tralitrala!
Und sitzt auf einem Steine da.

When Peter gladly would be going,
His trousers to the stone are
  growing;

The stuff is old, his heart is gay,
Young Peter tears himself away.

Nun möchte Peter sich erheben;
Die Hose bleibt am Steine kleben.

Der Stoff ist alt, die Lust ist groß;
Der Peter reißt sich wieder los.

Der Eispeter

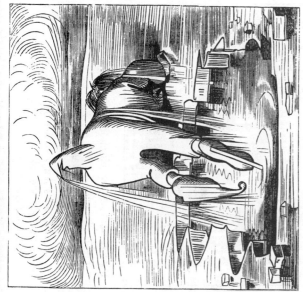

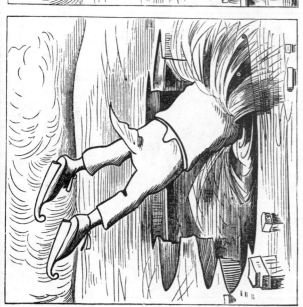

Just as I thought! here in a trice,
Has Peter fallen through the ice,

But with the loss of his new cap,
Friend Peter struggles from the
trap.

Na, richtig! Ja, ich dacht' es doch!
Da fällt er schon ins tiefe Loch.

Mit Hinterlassung seiner Mütze
Steigt Peter wieder aus der Pfütze.

Though small at first, there
    quickly grows,
A long ice-pendant on his nose.

Which lengthens fast, till by my
    life,
'Tis sharp as any butcher's knife!

Bald schießt hervor, obschon noch
    klein,
Ein Zacken Eis am Nasenbein.

Der Zacken wird noch immer besser
Und scharf als wie ein
    Schlachtermesser.

Der Eispeter

A mass of ice from head to toes,
He freezes faster as he goes.

And each one asks; "Who can this be?
'Tis a frozen porcupine I see?"

Der Zacken werden immer mehr,
Der Nasenzacken wird ein Speer.

Und jeder fragt: Wer mag das sein?
Das ist ja ein gefrornes
Stachelschwein!

Ice-Peter

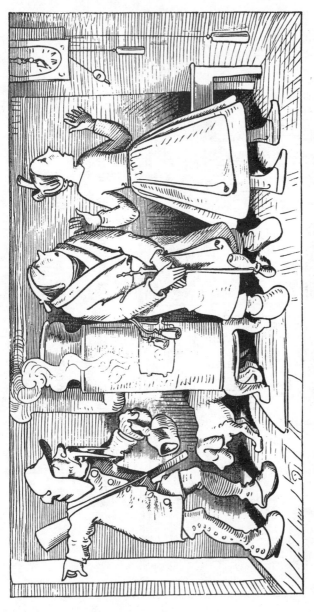

Oft at the clock his parents gaze,
And wonder where their Peter
stays.

Exclaims the Uncle, in a trice,
"I'll bet the rascal's on the ice!"

Die Eltern sehen nach der Uhr:
„Ach, ach! wo bleibt denn Peter
nur?"

Da ruft der Onkel in das Haus:
„Der Schlingel ist aufs Eis
hinaus!"

Der Eispeter

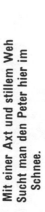

Mit einer Axt und stillem Weh
Sucht man den Peter hier im
   Schnee.

Schon sieht man mit betrübtem
   Blick
Ein Teil von Peters Kleidungsstück.

With sharpened axe and silent woe,
They seek for Peter 'mid the snow.

See how their anxious terror grows
To find a piece of Peter's clothes.

Much greater is their grief, I ween,   Doch größer war die Trauer da,
When Peter's very self is seen.   Als man den Peter selber sah.

Der Eispeter

Here Peter's carried home at last,
His father weeps, the tears freeze
fast.

Hier wird der Peter transportiert,
Der Vater weint, die Träne friert.

Beside the stove and teapot spout,
They lay the boy to thaw him out.

Behutsam läßt man Peters Glieder
Zu Haus am warmen Ofen nieder.

Der Eispeter

Hurrah! how grateful are their hearts;
The ice gives way, the water starts!

Juchhe! Die Freudigkeit ist groß;
Das Wasser rinnt, das Eis geht los.

Alas! alas! alack-a-day!
Poor boy, he's melted quite away.

Ach, aber ach! Nun ist's vorbei!
Der ganze Kerl zerrinnt zu Brei.

Here in a pickle-jar inter they
Peter, of better burial worthy.

Hier wird in einem Topf gefüllt
Des Peters traurig Ebenbild.

Yes, yes! within this earthen jar,
Poor Pete's remains preserved are.

The rebel, who at first was hard,
As soft as butter now, is jarred.

Ja, ja! in diesem Topf aus Stein,
Da machte man den Peter ein,

Der, nachdem er anfangs hart,
Später weich wie Butter ward.

VIII

THE BOY AND THE PIPE

The Story of the Disobedient Boy Who Would Smoke His Father's Pipe

(Krischan mit der Piepe:*
Eine Rauchphantasie)

Translated by Abby Langdon Alger

* This is the only piece Busch wrote entirely in *Plattdeutsch*. The reader will see that he was as nimble with it as with *Hochdeutsch*.

167

The father says: "I'm going out!
Christian! don't pull my pipe
  about!"

No sooner has he closed the door,
Than on the pipe is Christian's paw.

De Vader segt: „Ick mot nu
  gahn!
Krischan! lat de Piepen stahn!"

Kum awer geiht he ut der Doer,
Kriegt Krischan all de Piepen her.

Krischan mit der Piepe

Fie, Christian! what a dirty trick
Tobacco in your mouth to stick.

Why, zounds!—He's smoking, I
declare;
And what stirs in the corner there.

Min Krischan steckt ok gar nich
fuul
De Smoekepiepen in dat Muul,

He smoekt! – Wat, Deuker, is
denn dat?!
Mi dücht, dar achter rögt sick wat.

Th' umbrella dances with the
    sticks,
And with the tongs, the stove plays
    tricks.

De Stock is mit den Schirm in
    Gange,
De Aben danzet mit der Tange.

The coat is waltzing with the chair,

The table with the sofa there.

De Slaprock danzt mit den Stohl,
juheh!

Un de Disch mit den olen Kanapee.

All of a sudden—puff—it's dark:

Some demon sure is on a lark.

Up eenmal – puff! – do werd et dunkel:

Dat is de ole Runkelmunkel.

And puff—in floats as large as
life—
A second imp, the former's wife.

Un – puff! – kummt no'n Keerel
an:
Dat is de swarte Morian.

The Boy and the Pipe

Madly dance the pair and frolic,

Christian feels most melancholic.

Se danzet un springet un dreihet sick,

Den Krischan werd so wunderlick.

Krischan mit der Piepe

They whirl and shout with frantic
glee;
The room and Christian are at sea.

Se danzet, dildi, se trampelt,
schrum, schrum!
Wupp! dreiht sick de ganze Stube
um!

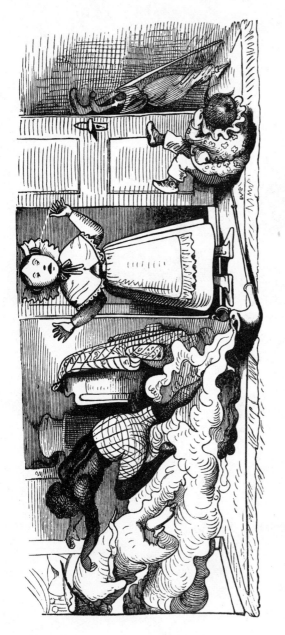

His mother opens wide the door,
And finds her Christian on the
floor.

Jüst tret de Moder in de Doer,
De Krischan ligt ganz krumm un
quer.

Krischan mit der Piepe

In bed he lies; the demons leer,
While mother stands with coffee
near.

He ligt to Bed; de Keerels winkt,
Als Moder swarten Kaffe bringt.

177

The strong black coffee down he drinks,

'T will do poor Christian good, methinks.

He drinkt den swarten Kaffe ut,

Dat deiht min lewen Krischan gut.

Krischan mit der Piepe

His father sits and smiles, and says:
"A warning this from evil ways!

"Ay, ay, my boy! in future, you
Will do as you are bid to do!!"

Un Vader sitt dabi un lacht
Un segt: „Dat heb ick lange
      dacht!

Ja, ja, min Jung! so mot et gahn!
Krischan, lat de Piepe stahn!!"

179

IX

FIRM FAITH

(*Fester Glauben*)

Teacher: "... and now I want to prove this theorem."
Pupil: "Why bother to prove it, teacher? I take your word for it."

Professor: „... Und nun will ich Ihnen diesen Lehrsatz jetzt auch beweisen."
Junge: „Wozu beweisen, Herr Professor? Ich glaub' es Ihnen so."

More Miscellaneous Mischief-makers:

Approximately Animal

X

THE TWO DUCKS AND THE FROG

(*Die beiden Enten und der Frosch*)

Translated, freely, by H. Arthur Klein

See here—two ducklings, young and
   fond
Are heading quickly for the pond.

Sieh' da zwei Enten jung und schön,
Die wollen an den Teich hingehn.

Oh, no, indeed, they're not
   spelunking;
You see, they find their food by
   dunking.

Zum Teiche gehn sie munter
Und tauchen die Köpfe unter.

The Two Ducks and the Frog

One duckling brings a fine green
  frog
Right from the bottom of the bog.

Die eine in der Goschen
Trägt einen grünen Froschen.

She thinks it would be quite a treat
This frog, all by herself, to eat.

Sie denkt allein ihn zu verschlingen.
Das soll ihr aber nicht gelingen.

Die beiden Enten und der Frosch

But both the ducklings, she and he,
Tug at the frog horrendously.

Die Ente und der Enterich,
Die ziehn den Frosch ganz
   fürchterlich.

They stretch him out far sideways,
   too;
If he weren't green, he'd look
   quite blue.

Sie ziehn ihn in die Quere,
Das tut ihm weh gar sehre.

The Two Ducks and the Frog

The frog fights bravely, like a man. (We'd like to help him—but who can?)	Der Frosch kämpft tapfer wie ein Mann. Ob das ihm wohl was helfen kann?

When one duck gets him by the head, The other grabs her crop instead.	Schon hat die eine ihn beim Kopf, Die andre hält ihr zu den Kropf.

Die beiden Enten und der Frosch

And while they're fighting that-a-
    way,
The froggie makes his getaway.

Die beiden Enten raufen,
Da hat der Frosch gut laufen.

This didn't get them anything;
Now they seek froggie in the
    spring.

Die Enten haben sich besunnen,
Und suchen den Frosch im
    Brunnen.

The Two Ducks and the Frog

But, after many a narrow scrape
The frog again makes his escape.

Sie suchen ihn im Wasserrohr,
Der Frosch springt aber schnell
  hervor.

Now, hear the quaking, quacking
  din,
For froggie's free, while they are
  IN!

Die Enten mit Geschnatter
Strecken die Köpfe durchs Gatter.

Die beiden Enten und der Frosch

Now froggie's gone! Each captive duck
Squawks fearfully, but still stays stuck.

Der Frosch ist fort – die Enten,
Wenn die nur auch fort könnten!

The cook, attracted by the row,
Grabs both and laughs: "I've got you now!"

Da kommt der Koch herbei sogleich
Und lacht: „Hehe, jetzt hab' ich euch!"

The frog was sick three weeks—
 no joking!—
But now—praise be!—he's back to
 smoking.

Drei Wochen war der Frosch so
 krank!
Jetzt raucht er wieder, Gott sei
 Dank!

CAT AND MOUSE

The Story of a Persistent Pussy Pursuing Her Prey

(*Katze und Maus:*

Eine Bilderposse)

Translated, freely, by H. Arthur Klein

Scene of Action: The Kitchen.
Left—a mouse hole.
Right—a hole in a boot. A pump.
A clotheshorse, on which hangs
a pair of trousers. A stable
lantern and a box of blacking.

Ort der Handlung: Die Küche
Links ein Mauseloch.
Rechts ein Loch im Stiefel. Eine
Pumpe. Ein Kleiderstock, woran
eine Hose hängt. Eine Stallaterne
und ein Topf mit Wichse.

Katze und Maus

Die Maus spaziert in die Laterne,
Der böse Kater sieht's von ferne.

Schnapp! springt er zu: das Glas
  zerbricht;
Die Maus, die kriegt er aber nicht.

The lantern's door here stands ajar;
The cat is watching from afar.

The cat jumps now! The glass is
  shot!
Has cat caught mouse? No, he has
  not. . .

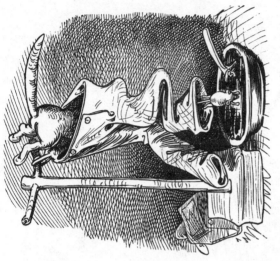

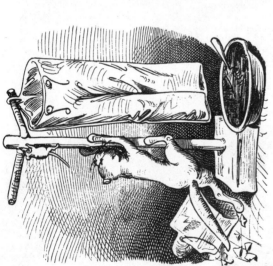

Miss Mouse goes dashing up the pole;
The cat's behind her, heart and soul!

On, through the pants, with pluck and luck!
The mouse is out; the cat seems stuck. . .

Den Kleiderstock erklimmt die Maus,
Der Kater nach in einem Saus.

Hier sausen sie durchs Hosenbein,
Die Maus heraus, die Katz' hinein.

Katze und Maus

The cat head-first, a live pile-
     driver,
Batters boot-blacking like a diver.

The cat is now half black as soot;
The mouse is leaping for the boot.

Klatsch! fällt der Kater mit dem
     Kopf
In einen schwarzen Wichsetopf.

Der Kater ist ein halber Mohr,
Die Maus springt in das Stiefelrohr.

195

"I'll get you yet!" the tomcat
   thinks,
But boots sometimes have handy
   chinks. . . .

Here Mousie jumps quite clear of
   that
Old boot, which looks like Pussy's
   hat!

Der Kater denkt: „Dich krieg ich
   noch!"
Der Stiefel aber hat ein Loch.

Hier springt denn auch die gute
   Maus
Bereits zum Stiefelloch heraus.

Katze und Maus

Die Maus läuft schnell ins
   Mäusenest;
Der Kater sitzt im Stiefel fest.

Ja, stelle dich nur auf den Kopf!
Der Stiefel bleibt dir doch am
   Schopf.

The mouse runs swiftly to her nest;
The tomcat in the boot is pressed.

Yes, just try standing upside
   down!
The boot's still sticking to your
   crown!

Both Cook and Hostler gaze aghast
On what's transpired here at last...

Die Köchin und der Hausknecht sehn
Mit Staunen an, was hier geschehn.

And, as you see, their strain is great
The cat and boot to separate.

Und beide sieht man mit Bemühn
Am Katzenschwanz und Stiefel
ziehn.

"Migosh, we've done it, after all!"
And flat upon the ground both
fall!

Pardauz! Da haben wir es ja!
Sie liegen alle beide da.

Katze und Maus

The cat, hard pressed, a rank offender,
Becomes a beaten bitter-ender!

Der Kater, der's verdient gehabt,
Wird eingeklemmt und abgeklappt!

And if you're black, back where you sit,
With water you get rid of it. . .

Und wenn sich einer schwarz gemacht,
Mit Wasser wird's herausgebracht.

Katze und Maus

The mice, however, make a ring
And dance about and loudly sing:

"The boot has worn its toe away!
Long live the boot! Hip-hip-
      hooray!"

Die Mäuse aber springen
Im Kreis herum und singen:

„Der brave Stiefel hat ein Loch!
Der Stiefel lebe! Vivat hoch!"

AFTERWORD

The following notes and observations are offered in the hope of increasing enjoyment and understanding—in that order —but they are by no means urged upon the reader. If such editorial apparatus were *essential,* the justification for a representative selection of Busch in English would be largely non-existent.

These notes apply directly or indirectly to the twin texts: German original and English translation. They do not attempt to offer a biography of that cryptic, strange, and to some extent sick, personality: Wilhelm Busch. Nor do they offer an over-all evaluation of his place in the literature of German-speaking lands, or the full history of the various translations of Busch works into English on both sides of the Atlantic. For such discussion there may be opportunity elsewhere.

I. MAX AND MORITZ

Max and Moritz: This famous title appeared altered to *Max and Maurice* when the Charles T. Brooks translation, here reprinted, was first published in 1871. *Moritz* has here been restored throughout—the only change made in the Brooks text. The names of this infamous pair have undergone strange metamorphoses as the scamps have entered world literature in translation and perpetrated their outrages in millions of copies sold in many lands. *Notl un Motl* they became in a Yiddish translation by Joseph Tunkel, published 1929 in Warsaw. They appeared as *Corococó e Carracacá* in Portuguese in a 1943 Brazilian publication; and as *Jake un Johnny* in a Pennsylvania Dutch version by J. W. Frey, 1943.

Among their most recent transformations has been the change to Gad and Dan in a Hebrew translation by Anda Amir (Pinkerfeld), published by Niv in Tel Aviv, 1956. The full title transliterated is: GAD V'DAN SHISHA TA'ALLULIM SHEL SHNAY SHOVAVIM. Other renamings are interesting: the peasant has become Judah; Uncle Fritz appears as Mordecai; and Tailor Böck is Tayash. The fourth trick is omitted and the conclusion is altered: the two malefactors are taken to a mountain and there hanged.

Afterword

Even before Winnie the Pooh and Christopher Robin, Max
and Moritz had been latinized. Three different Latin translations
have appeared. The first, by G. Merten, published 1932 in
Munich, Germany, and now out of print, was entitled *Max et
Moritz, facinora puerilia septem dolis fraudibusque peracta; in
sermonem Latinum conversa a versificatore sereno.* Another,
by E. Steindl, published by the same Munich house in 1953,
bears a 1925 copyright date. The full title is: *Max et Moritz
puerorum facinora scurrilia septem fabellis, quarum materiam
repperit depinxitque Gulielmus Busch, demonstrata isdem versibus,
quibus auctor Latine reddidit Ervinus Steindl, Carantanus.* The
third Latin translation, by Paoli, appeared 1959 in Florence,
Italy. The title: *Willelmus Busch, Maximi et Mauritii malefacta.
Ab Hugone Henrico Paoli Latinis versibus enarrata. F. Le Monnier
Florentiae.* Where the Steindl version had used the eight-
syllabled, strongly rhythmed rhyming style of medieval Latin,
Paoli chose the classical hexameter.

But there is still another memorial to Max and Moritz, many
times more important than the varied translations, if we take
mass distribution into account. This memorial may be viewed
any Sunday in popular American funny-papers. Direct des-
cendants of M. and M. are Hans and Fritz in two long-established
Sunday comics: *The Katzenjammer Kids* and *The Captain and
the Kids.* This line of the family was created in 1897 by Rudolph
Dirks, pioneer of the "slam-bang-pow" school of American
funnies.*

As general editor of this volume and its "sister" volume,
Hypocritical Helena, I felt that both books and readers would
gain if some, at least, of the included translations were by others
than the Kleins, H. A. and M. C. Accordingly, here is Brooks'
version of *Max und Moritz.* (Subsequent pages include three of
Abby Langdon Alger's translations of shorter pieces.)

The slender brown book bearing Brooks' translation
appeared in Boston in 1871. Since *Max und Moritz* was first
published mid-year of 1865 in Munich, Brooks must have been
at work putting it into English within four or five years after the

---

*The fuller story of the *Max and Moritz* influence on American funnies
need not be retold here. It may be found in Stephen Becker's *Comic Art in
America,* N.Y., 1959, page 14; in Martin Sheridan's *Comics and Their Creators,*
Boston, 1942, page 58; and in Colton Waugh's *The Comics,* N.Y., 1947, page 10.
It is a fascinating story of sources, modifications, conflicts, and developments
in one of our lively arts. Based on it, we may well call W. Busch the stepfather,
if not the father, of an important group of comics in the United States.

first copies could have reached him in the United States; unless, of course, he first met Max and Moritz on a visit to Germany.

In any case, this appears to be the first complete Englishing of the most famous of Busch's picture stories. In fact, it is one of the first published English translations of Busch material. Three years earlier, 1868, in London, had appeared a work entitled *A Bushel of Merry-Thoughts,* translated by W. Harry Rogers. The verses were basically Rogers, however, rather than Busch. Included were verses based on three of the picture series to be found elsewhere in this book under the titles of *The Egghead and the Two Cut-ups of Corinth, Cat and Mouse,* and *Ice-Peter.* These plus another, titled there *Sugar-Bread,* made up the complete contents of this early Busch-in-English. The Brooks translation of *Max und Moritz* thus has a substantial priority.

Charles Timothy Brooks (1813-1883) was a distinguished, if not a great translator. Prior to *Max and Maurice,* his translations had included a 273-page collection of *German Lyrics* by various poets (1853); the novel *Titan* by Jean Paul Richter (1862); and (in 1863) *The Jobsiad: a grotesco-comico-heroic poem from the German of Dr. Arnold Kortum,* also known as *The Life, opinions, actions, and fate of Hieronimus Jobs, the candidate.* Brooks also translated much, though not all, of Goethe's *Faust.* Unfortunately, his work was overshadowed by the later (1870-71) *Faust* translation of Bayard Taylor (1825-1878). Taylor's translation adhered to Goethe's varying meters and provided readers with richer fare than Brooks' efforts.

Brooks deserves to be remembered as a pioneer and devoted intermediary of cultural exchange. An attempt to do him rather belated justice was the publication sponsored by the Modern Languages Association: *Charles Timothy Brooks, Translator from German, and the Genteel Tradition,* by Camillo von Klenze, 114 pages, D. C. Heath & Co., 1937.

Before locating the Brooks translation I had made my own version of the Preface to *Max und Moritz.* For whatever interest it may offer, this is it:

> How often one must read or hear
> Of children, who should be so dear,
> But are as naughty as can be
> And practice darkest deviltry . . .

Afterword

Like this rare pair of lads so bad
Named Max and Moritz . . . Truly sad
The way they flouted what was right,
Committing mischief day and night.

Believe me, it would really hurt you
To see them scoff and mock at virtue,
And, at almost any time,
Concoct a new and shocking crime . . .
Tease and torment man and beast . . .
Steal fresh fruit and have a feast . . .

Alas, all that's a lot more fun
Than getting schoolwork wisely done
And sitting still in front of Teacher,
Or in the church to please the preacher.

But when their dreadful end I see,
I must cry "Ouch!" for agony.
Yes, I must wince for pain, pain, pain,
When I gaze ahead again . . .

For to a truly sorry pass
Did Max and Moritz come at last!
And so we here have illustrated
Just what these terrors perpetrated.

First Trick

Ach herrje, herrjemine! Herrje is a rather obvious euphemism or
masking for *Herr Jesu! Herrjemine* probably started out as a
substitute for *Herr Jesu mein!* Busch had abundant supplies
of expletives, which he used with dexterity and gusto, thus
bringing into his texts some of the same dynamics and
slapdash that he achieved in his drawings.

Second Trick

Wenn er wieder aufgewärmt: An example of an occurrence—or
non-occurrence—extremely common in Busch's jingles;
namely, the omission of the inflected form of the auxiliary
verbs *sein* (to be) and *haben* (to have) from the end of
dependent clauses. The effect is to make the passages more

Afterword

colloquial and informal. Here we understand: *Wenn er wieder aufgewärmt (ist).*

Third Trick

"Come out, you buck! . . . muck! muck! muck!" In the German, the rascals had called the tailor a *Bock (Böck)*—a he-goat; and *meck* is the normal word for the sound made by a goat.

Die Brücke bricht in Stücke: Example of internal rhyme, rather infrequent in Busch.

Übrigens bei alledem Ist so etwas nicht bequem: An example of the numerous pat, proverblike couplets that make Busch so delightful in German. Lines like these are consummately quotable on many occasions of daily life!

Fourth Trick

With the clerical profession Smoking always was a passion: Lämpel, though he played organ in church, was not a "cleric," as Brooks' translation might suggest. He was a teacher. Possibly he also doubled as lay pastor in the church. Also, Busch did not generalize that smoking was the passion of Lämpel's whole profession; he wrote only that "this good teacher was an admirer of tobacco." By that he meant that Lämpel was a devotee, as indeed Busch himself was—a tobacco fiend, who smoked like a furnace or like a Mark Twain, and who more than once became sick with nicotine poisoning.

Fifth Trick

Fidibus: A spill; that is, a twist of paper or sliver of wood, such as was used for lighting candles, or—and this is the use implied here—pipes. Busch, though never husband or father, was an active, practicing uncle. The latter part of his long life was spent with his widowed sister, Frau Fanny Nöldeke, and her three sons, Herman, Adolf, and Otto Nöldeke. In many ways he acted as a father to these nephews, and they displayed toward him and, later, toward his memory, a truly filial devotion. Together they authored the first important biographical work on Busch, published in 1909, the year after his death. Their attitude was naturally protective and laudatory.

Afterword

Guckste wohl! This does not have the slightest resemblance to
O be joyful! supplied by Brooks. It stands for *Guckst du
wohl,* or "Just take a good look!"

Last Trick

Maltersäcke: The archaic word *Malter* applied to a measure of
capacity, used for grain. It was equal to about 150 litres.

The corn runs out: It would be a mistake to assume that this is
our corn or "maize." German *das Korn* ordinarily indicates
a grain such as wheat.

"Zapperment!" An expletive only slightly disguising its origin
in an oath by the Blessed Sacrament.

"Dat Ding werd lichter!" The peasant—or farmer—is here
speaking his native Plattdeutsch, the dialect familiar to
Busch in the state of Hannover where he grew up and lived
most of his life. In "Hochdeutsch" the exclamation would
be *Das Ding wird leichter!* Either way it means "This thing is
getting lighter!" Translator Brooks, in order to arrive at
"I see where it lies!" must have assumed that the *lichter*
referred to a growing *light* (of comprehension) which
permits the farmer to see what had been hidden from him
before.

II. KER AND PLUNK

Plisch und Plum, the original of this translation, was first
published in 1882. It thus appeared about 17 years after *Max und
Moritz* and about five years after *Hypocritical Helena (Die Fromme
Helene),* which forms the pièce de résistance of the sister volume
to the present book. *Plisch und Plum,* in terms of drawing and
text, represented a more mature and developed Busch, one who
had behind him successful years of planning and executing
picture stories for book publication.

It is conceivable that, since *Max and Moritz,* the most
successful of his works in terms of continuing total sales, had
been built around a mischievous or unruly pair, Busch may have
set out to double the dose—two pairs, one of boys, the other of
dogs. They begin as disruptive demons, thorns in the side of the
Established Order. However, the passing years in some respects
had developed a milder and gentler mood in Busch. So Paul and

Afterword

Peter and their two dogs are not made to suffer grim ends. Instead— but that is all told in the picture story itself . . .

(Charles T. Brooks, translator of *Max and Maurice,* wrote a translation of this work also. The book, published in 1882 by Roberts Brothers, Boston, under the title of *Plish and Plum,* bears the copyright date 1871. Thus, Brooks must have completed his version the same year that the original by Busch was published in Germany. Space and time do not permit comparison here of key passages in the two versions; I would say here only that Brooks' *Plish and Plum* impresses me as a better, more subtle and animated translation than his *Max and Maurice.* Some passages, in fact, made me feel, "I wish we had thought of *that!*" Others, however, made me think smugly, "Glad we didn't do *that!*")

Chapter One

Plisch! . . . *Plum!* The double splashing sound, equivalent to English *kerplunk* or *kersplash!* The German form provided the names for the two dogs, and the same principle has been followed in providing the English names.

Chapter Four

Gaudium : Latin for "joy, pleasure." The colloquial and dialectal German word *Gaudi,* meaning "fun" or "spree," comes from *gaudium,* probably via the schoolroom.

Chapter Five

This short chapter is omitted here because it unfortunately embodies some of the anti-Semitism which tainted the work of Busch from time to time. There is no need for reproducing such occurrences in this day and age.

Chapter Seven

"Tugend will ermuntert sein, Bosheit kann man schon allein!" Almost everyone who has spent time with Busch has his favorite quotable couplets. This is one of mine.

Magister Bockelmann : The indication here is that he is Master of Arts *(Artium Magister).* Of just what sort of arts, we shall see soon enough.

Afterword

nunmehro: Archaic form of *nunmehr,* an adverb meaning "at present, now." Master B.'s talk to the boys is interlarded with antiquated and pedantic terms.

alldieweil: From *dieweil,* a rare adverb and conjunction meaning "while, as long as, meanwhile."

Conclusion

Comes this Mister, known as "Hope": Mister Pief, or Hope, as he is named in the translation, is really an old familiar friend in new guise. He is that imperturbable, unbudgeable eccentric Englishman, known as Phineas Fogg in Jules Verne's *Around the World in Eighty Days.* He is so rich and so confident of his essential rightness, based on the might of the then dominant British Empire, that he can afford to be eccentric even when travelling in the unfamiliar territory of Hannover, Germany.

As envy grips his heart: Schlee-Schlich has envied himself into the watery death he had intended for the two dogs. So the picture story ends in an outburst of poetic justice and with a last curling wisp of smoke to sign it off.

III. THE EGGHEAD AND THE TWO CUT-UPS OF CORINTH

This piece was first published 1862 in the *Münchener Bilderbogen,* and was later included in the book *Schnaken und Schnurren,* 1867.

"Ja, ja! Das kommt von das!" Busch is fond of making his stuffed-shirt characters utter the most obscure banalities with an air of deep wisdom.

IV. THE RAVEN-ROBBIN' RASCALS

This piece was first published 1861 in the *Münchener Bilderbogen,* and was later included in the book *Schnaken und Schnurren,* 1867. These verses differ in rhythm from most of those that Busch wrote for his later and longer picture stories such as *Max and Moritz* and *Hypocritical Helena.* The latter has almost all four-stressed lines, while some of these are three-stressed. Their effect is accordingly somewhat more juvenile and jumpy.

Gewest: In place of the formal *gewesen.*

Afterword

V. DECEITFUL HENRY

This piece was first published 1864 in the *Münchener Bilderbogen,* and was later included in the book *Schnaken und Schnurren,* 1867.

Nimm diese Brezen: The *Brezen* is the ancestor of the familiar pretzel. The latter seems to have shrunk drastically since crossing the Atlantic.

Here Henry's fallen: The style and spirit of the drawings in this sequence are reminiscent of the familiar, older, and cruder picture-poem series entitled *Der Struwwelpeter* by Dr. Heinrich Hoffman. That direly didactic work, intended for the edification and terrorizing of the young, was created less than twenty years prior to this series by Busch.

VI. THE BOY AND THE POPGUN

This was first published in 1868, as one of a group entitled *Bildergeschichten* (Picture Stories). The title should be *The Boy and the Peashooter,* or *Blowgun.*

Abby Langdon Alger's translation, here reprinted, appeared under the English title used here in a volume published 1880 in New York, entitled *The Mischief Book.* Its title page identified William Busch as "author of Max and Maurice," probably a reference to the title of C. T. Brooks' book, published less than ten years earlier.

Abby Langdon Alger herself (born in 1850) translated several German works into English, among them two books about the composer Schumann: *R. Schumann, sein Leben und seine Werke,* by A. Reissman; and *R. Schumann, eine Biographie,* by W. Wasiliewski. She also translated the *Undine* of Baron Friedrich Heinrich Karl de la Motte Fouqué (1777–1843).

Her skill as a translator of Busch seems distinctly inferior to that of Brooks. From time to time she misses an important point completely, and many of her rhymes are attained at excessive cost in terms of meaning, word order, and rhythm. In the best of Busch, like the best of W. S. Gilbert and other masters of light, humorous verse, rhyme is a joy, a jollity, a delightful word-play that mingles fun and pun. Rarely, in the German, does Busch seem forced or oppressed by the demands of rhyming. If a translation seems so, then to that extent, at least, it is unBuschian.

213

Afterword

And dips his pretzel in his tea: Actually, Herr Bartelmann is almost certainly taking coffee.

Drum schiess . . . Auf keine alten Leute nicht! Note the humorously colloquial double negative: *keine . . . nicht.*

VII. ICE-PETER

This was first published 1864 in the book *Bilderpossen,* a collection subtitled "stories for children who like to laugh." *The Story of the Foolish Boy Who Would Go Skating* was the subtitle used in the Alger translation as it appeared in *The Mischief Book* of 1880.

Old Uncle Forster: Der Onkel Förster actually signifies "his uncle, the forester (or game warden)." The fact that this man is an official, not just an ordinary old uncle, makes a great deal of difference psychologically in the mental world we are visiting here. He is not simply a friendly neighbor or relative; he is the very Voice of Experience and Authority, to defy whom, in the ideological world of Wilhelm Busch, is sure to bring drastic or even fatal consequences.

Da machte man den Peter ein: The verb *einmachen* is deadly accurate, for it means "to put up" (as preserves) or "to pickle."

VIII. THE BOY AND THE PIPE

This was first published 1864 as part of the book *Bilderpossen.* The title and subtitle given here in English are as they appeared in the Alger translation in *The Mischief Book,* 1880. This piece was conceived and written by Busch in the Plattdeutsch spoken in his part of Hannover.

Piepe: Hochdeutsch *Pfeife* (pipe). As so often, the Plattdeutsch word is noticeably closer in sound to its English counterpart than is the Hochdeutsch equivalent.

Christian's paw: No implications as to Christian's bestiality; just a matter of making a rhyme the hard way.

The coat is waltzing: In this and the following drawings, motion increases and takes over throughout the scene. In the draughtsmanship of his later years, Busch became more fluid and simple in the delineation and suggestion of people and things in violent motion.

De ole Runkelmunkel: Old Runkel-Munkel, a popular familiar spirit, apparently both feared and favored.

A second imp, the former's wife: Imp No. Two is actually a male, and was possibly converted by Alger into a "wife" only for the sake of a rhyme. I offer the following rectification and consolation prize to Imp No. Two:

> And—puff!—here comes another one:
> A Nubian named Morian.

"A warning this from evil ways!" What Father said, in Plattdeutsch, was actually "I've long suspected this," or, "I've been thinking this a long time." The "warning from evil ways" was Translator Alger's injection. And in the following couplet, Father did not predict that Christian would always do what he was told; rather he simply repeated what he had said at the very beginning: "Christian, let be the pipe!"

IX. FIRM FAITH

This is a sample of single-panel humorous drawings, such as Busch occasionally turned out for *Fliegende Blätter* during the period 1859–1871. This one appeared in 1863. It is typical not so much of the work for which Busch became famous as of the sort of thing he moved away from when he developed his picture stories with structure, episodes, continuing characters, etc.

X. THE TWO DUCKS AND THE FROG

This was first published 1861 in the *Münchener Bilderbogen,* and was included in the 1867 book *Schnaken und Schnurren.*

But now—praise be!—he's back to smoking: When Busch himself fell ill, the harbinger of returning health was always his resumption of his inveterate smoking. And he doubtless said "Gott sei Dank!" himself on such occasions.

XI. CAT AND MOUSE

This was first published 1864 in the book collection *Bilderpossen.*

Pardauz! An expletive apparently growing out of a euphemism for *par Dieu!*

Afterword

"Vivat hoch!" Hoch soll er leben! would be more completely Germanized. And what could provide a more suitable ending for these assorted afterwords than the joyous outcry which has been translated as

Hip-hip-hooray!

H. ARTHUR KLEIN

A CATALOGUE OF SELECTED DOVER BOOKS
IN ALL FIELDS OF INTEREST

A CATALOGUE OF SELECTED DOVER BOOKS
IN ALL FIELDS OF INTEREST

THE NOTEBOOKS OF LEONARDO DA VINCI, edited by J.P. Richter. Extracts from manuscripts reveal great genius; on painting, sculpture, anatomy, sciences, geography, etc. Both Italian and English. 186 ms. pages reproduced, plus 500 additional drawings, including studies for Last Supper, Sforza monument, etc. 860pp. 7⅞ x 10¾.   USO 22572-0, 22573-9 Pa., Two vol. set $15.90

ART NOUVEAU DESIGNS IN COLOR, Alphonse Mucha, Maurice Verneuil, Georges Auriol. Full-color reproduction of Combinaisons ornamentales (c. 1900) by Art Nouveau masters. Floral, animal, geometric, interlacings, swashes — borders, frames, spots — all incredibly beautiful. 60 plates, hundreds of designs. 9⅜ x 8¹/₁₆.   22885-1 Pa. $4.00

GRAPHIC WORKS OF ODILON REDON. All great fantastic lithographs, etchings, engravings, drawings, 209 in all. Monsters, Huysmans, still life work, etc. Introduction by Alfred Werner. 209pp. 9⅛ x 12¼.   21996-8 Pa. $6.00

EXOTIC FLORAL PATTERNS IN COLOR, E.-A. Seguy. Incredibly beautiful full-color pochoir work by great French designer of 20's. Complete Bouquets et frondaisons, Suggestions pour étoffes. Richness must be seen to be believed. 40 plates containing 120 patterns. 80pp. 9⅜ x 12¼.   23041-4 Pa. $6.00

SELECTED ETCHINGS OF JAMES A. McN. WHISTLER, James A. McN. Whistler. 149 outstanding etchings by the great American artist, including selections from the Thames set and two Venice sets, the complete French set, and many individual prints. Introduction and explanatory note on each print by Maria Naylor. 157pp. 9⅜ x 12¼.   23194-1 Pa. $5.00

VISUAL ILLUSIONS: THEIR CAUSES, CHARACTERISTICS, AND APPLICATIONS, Matthew Luckiesh. Thorough description, discussion; shape and size, color, motion; natural illusion. Uses in art and industry. 100 illustrations. 252pp.
21530-X Pa. $3.00

TEN BOOKS ON ARCHITECTURE, Vitruvius. The most important book ever written on architecture. Early Roman aesthetics, technology, classical orders, site selection, all other aspects. Stands behind everything since. Morgan translation. 331pp.
20645-9 Pa. $3.75

THE CODEX NUTTALL, A PICTURE MANUSCRIPT FROM ANCIENT MEXICO, as first edited by Zelia Nuttall. Only inexpensive edition, in full color, of a pre-Columbian Mexican (Mixtec) book. 88 color plates show kings, gods, heroes, temples, sacrifices. New explanatory, historical introduction by Arthur G. Miller. 96pp. 11⅜ x 8½.   23168-2 Pa. $7.50

CREATIVE LITHOGRAPHY AND HOW TO DO IT, Grant Arnold. Lithography as art form: working directly on stone, transfer of drawings, lithotint, mezzotint, color printing; also metal plates. Detailed, thorough. 27 illustrations. 214pp.
21208-4 Pa. $3.50

DESIGN MOTIFS OF ANCIENT MEXICO, Jorge Enciso. Vigorous, powerful ceramic stamp impressions — Maya, Aztec, Toltec, Olmec. Serpents, gods, priests, dancers, etc. 153pp. 6⅛ x 9¼.
20084-1 Pa. $2.50

AMERICAN INDIAN DESIGN AND DECORATION, Leroy Appleton. Full text, plus more than 700 precise drawings of Inca, Maya, Aztec, Pueblo, Plains, NW Coast basketry, sculpture, painting, pottery, sand paintings, metal, etc. 4 plates in color. 279pp. 8⅜ x 11¼.
22704-9 Pa. $5.00

CHINESE LATTICE DESIGNS, Daniel S. Dye. Incredibly beautiful geometric designs: circles, voluted, simple dissections, etc. Inexhaustible source of ideas, motifs. 1239 illustrations. 469pp. 6⅛ x 9¼.
23096-1 Pa. $5.00

JAPANESE DESIGN MOTIFS, Matsuya Co. Mon, or heraldic designs. Over 4000 typical, beautiful designs: birds, animals, flowers, swords, fans, geometric; all beautifully stylized. 213pp. 11⅜ x 8¼.
22874-6 Pa. $5.00

PERSPECTIVE, Jan Vredeman de Vries. 73 perspective plates from 1604 edition; buildings, townscapes, stairways, fantastic scenes. Remarkable for beauty, surrealistic atmosphere; real eye-catchers. Introduction by Adolf Placzek. 74pp. 11⅜ x 8¼.
20186-4 Pa. $3.00

EARLY AMERICAN DESIGN MOTIFS. Suzanne E. Chapman. 497 motifs, designs, from painting on wood, ceramics, appliqué, glassware, samplers, metal work, etc. Florals, landscapes, birds and animals, geometrics, letters, etc. Inexhaustible. Enlarged edition. 138pp. 8⅜ x 11¼.
22985-8 Pa. $3.50
23084-8 Clothbd. $7.95

VICTORIAN STENCILS FOR DESIGN AND DECORATION, edited by E.V. Gillon, Jr. 113 wonderful ornate Victorian pieces from German sources; florals, geometrics; borders, corner pieces; bird motifs, etc. 64pp. 9⅜ x 12¼.
21995-X Pa. $3.00

ART NOUVEAU: AN ANTHOLOGY OF DESIGN AND ILLUSTRATION FROM THE STUDIO, edited by E.V. Gillon, Jr. Graphic arts: book jackets, posters, engravings, illustrations, decorations; Crane, Beardsley, Bradley and many others. Inexhaustible. 92pp. 8⅛ x 11.
22388-4 Pa. $2.50

ORIGINAL ART DECO DESIGNS, William Rowe. First-rate, highly imaginative modern Art Deco frames, borders, compositions, alphabets, florals, insectals, Wurlitzer-types, etc. Much finest modern Art Deco. 80 plates, 8 in color. 8⅜ x 11¼.
22567-4 Pa. $3.50

HANDBOOK OF DESIGNS AND DEVICES, Clarence P. Hornung. Over 1800 basic geometric designs based on circle, triangle, square, scroll, cross, etc. Largest such collection in existence. 261pp.
20125-2 Pa. $2.75

150 MASTERPIECES OF DRAWING, edited by Anthony Toney. 150 plates, early 15th century to end of 18th century; Rembrandt, Michelangelo, Dürer, Fragonard, Watteau, Wouwerman, many others. 150pp. 8⅜ x 11¼.   21032-4 Pa. $4.00

THE GOLDEN AGE OF THE POSTER, Hayward and Blanche Cirker. 70 extraordinary posters in full colors, from Maîtres de l'Affiche, Mucha, Lautrec, Bradley, Cheret, Beardsley, many others. 9⅜ x 12¼.   22753-7 Pa. $5.95

SIMPLICISSIMUS, selection, translations and text by Stanley Appelbaum. 180 satirical drawings, 16 in full color, from the famous German weekly magazine in the years 1896 to 1926. 24 artists included: Grosz, Kley, Pascin, Kubin, Kollwitz, plus Heine, Thöny, Bruno Paul, others. 172pp. 8½ x 12¼.   23098-8 Pa. $5.00
                                                         23099-6 Clothbd. $10.00

THE EARLY WORK OF AUBREY BEARDSLEY, Aubrey Beardsley. 157 plates, 2 in color: Manon Lescaut, Madame Bovary, Morte d'Arthur, Salome, other. Introduction by H. Marillier. 175pp. 8½ x 11.   21816-3 Pa. $4.00

THE LATER WORK OF AUBREY BEARDSLEY, Aubrey Beardsley. Exotic masterpieces of full maturity: Venus and Tannhäuser, Lysistrata, Rape of the Lock, Volpone, Savoy material, etc. 174 plates, 2 in color. 176pp. 8½ x 11.   21817-1 Pa. $4.50

DRAWINGS OF WILLIAM BLAKE, William Blake. 92 plates from Book of Job, Divine Comedy, Paradise Lost, visionary heads, mythological figures, Laocoön, etc. Selection, introduction, commentary by Sir Geoffrey Keynes. 178pp. 8½ x 11.
                                                         22303-5 Pa. $4.00

LONDON: A PILGRIMAGE, Gustave Doré, Blanchard Jerrold. Squalor, riches, misery, beauty of mid-Victorian metropolis; 55 wonderful plates, 125 other illustrations, full social, cultural text by Jerrold. 191pp. of text. 8⅛ x 11.
                                                         22306-X Pa. $6.00

THE COMPLETE WOODCUTS OF ALBRECHT DÜRER, edited by Dr. W. Kurth. 346 in all: Old Testament, St. Jerome, Passion, Life of Virgin, Apocalypse, many others. Introduction by Campbell Dodgson. 285pp. 8½ x 12¼.   21097-9 Pa. $6.00

THE DISASTERS OF WAR, Francisco Goya. 83 etchings record horrors of Napoleonic wars in Spain and war in general. Reprint of 1st edition, plus 3 additional plates. Introduction by Philip Hofer. 97pp. 9⅜ x 8¼.   21872-4 Pa. $3.50

ENGRAVINGS OF HOGARTH, William Hogarth. 101 of Hogarth's greatest works: Rake's Progress, Harlot's Progress, Illustrations for Hudibras, Midnight Modern Conversation, Before and After, Beer Street and Gin Lane, many more. Full commentary. 256pp. 11 x 14.   22479-1 Pa. $7.95

PRIMITIVE ART, Franz Boas. Great anthropologist on ceramics, textiles, wood, stone, metal, etc.; patterns, technology, symbols, styles. All areas, but fullest on Northwest Coast Indians. 350 illustrations. 378pp.   20025-6 Pa. $3.75

MOTHER GOOSE'S MELODIES. Facsimile of fabulously rare Munroe and Francis "copyright 1833" Boston edition. Familiar and unusual rhymes, wonderful old woodcut illustrations. Edited by E.F. Bleiler. 128pp. 4½ x 6⅜. 22577-1 Pa. $1.50

MOTHER GOOSE IN HIEROGLYPHICS. Favorite nursery rhymes presented in rebus form for children. Fascinating 1849 edition reproduced in toto, with key. Introduction by E.F. Bleiler. About 400 woodcuts. 64pp. 6⅞ x 5¼. 20745-5 Pa. $1.50

PETER PIPER'S PRACTICAL PRINCIPLES OF PLAIN & PERFECT PRONUNCIATION. Alliterative jingles and tongue-twisters. Reproduction in full of 1830 first American edition. 25 spirited woodcuts. 32pp. 4½ x 6⅜. 22560-7 Pa. $1.25

MARMADUKE MULTIPLY'S MERRY METHOD OF MAKING MINOR MATHEMATICIANS. Fellow to Peter Piper, it teaches multiplication table by catchy rhymes and woodcuts. 1841 Munroe & Francis edition. Edited by E.F. Bleiler. 103pp. 4⅝ x 6. 22773-1 Pa. $1.25

THE NIGHT BEFORE CHRISTMAS, Clement Moore. Full text, and woodcuts from original 1848 book. Also critical, historical material. 19 illustrations. 40pp. 4⅝ x 6. 22797-9 Pa. $1.35

THE KING OF THE GOLDEN RIVER, John Ruskin. Victorian children's classic of three brothers, their attempts to reach the Golden River, what becomes of them. Facsimile of original 1889 edition. 22 illustrations. 56pp. 4⅝ x 6⅜. 20066-3 Pa. $1.50

DREAMS OF THE RAREBIT FIEND, Winsor McCay. Pioneer cartoon strip, unexcelled for beauty, imagination, in 60 full sequences. Incredible technical virtuosity, wonderful visual wit. Historical introduction. 62pp. 8⅜ x 11¼. 21347-1 Pa. $2.50

THE KATZENJAMMER KIDS, Rudolf Dirks. In full color, 14 strips from 1906-7; full of imagination, characteristic humor. Classic of great historical importance. Introduction by August Derleth. 32pp. 9¼ x 12¼. 23005-8 Pa. $2.00

LITTLE ORPHAN ANNIE AND LITTLE ORPHAN ANNIE IN COSMIC CITY, Harold Gray. Two great sequences from the early strips: our curly-haired heroine defends the Warbucks' financial empire and, then, takes on meanie Phineas P. Pinchpenny. Leapin' lizards! 178pp. 6⅛ x 8⅜. 23107-0 Pa. $2.00

ABSOLUTELY MAD INVENTIONS, A.E. Brown, H.A. Jeffcott. Hilarious, useless, or merely absurd inventions all granted patents by the U.S. Patent Office. Edible tie pin, mechanical hat tipper, etc. 57 illustrations. 125pp. 22596-8 Pa. $1.50

THE DEVIL'S DICTIONARY, Ambrose Bierce. Barbed, bitter, brilliant witticisms in the form of a dictionary. Best, most ferocious satire America has produced. 145pp. 20487-1 Pa. $1.75

THE BEST DR. THORNDYKE DETECTIVE STORIES, R. Austin Freeman. The Case of Oscar Brodski, The Moabite Cipher, and 5 other favorites featuring the great scientific detective, plus his long-believed-lost first adventure — 31 New Inn — reprinted here for the first time. Edited by E.F. Bleiler. USO 20388-3 Pa. $3.00

BEST "THINKING MACHINE" DETECTIVE STORIES, Jacques Futrelle. The Problem of Cell 13 and 11 other stories about Prof. Augustus S.F.X. Van Dusen, including two "lost" stories. First reprinting of several. Edited by E.F. Bleiler. 241pp. 20537-1 Pa. $3.00

UNCLE SILAS, J. Sheridan LeFanu. Victorian Gothic mystery novel, considered by many best of period, even better than Collins or Dickens. Wonderful psychological terror. Introduction by Frederick Shroyer. 436pp. 21715-9 Pa. $4.50

BEST DR. POGGIOLI DETECTIVE STORIES, T.S. Stribling. 15 best stories from EQMM and The Saint offer new adventures in Mexico, Florida, Tennessee hills as Poggioli unravels mysteries and combats Count Jalacki. 217pp. 23227-1 Pa. $3.00

EIGHT DIME NOVELS, selected with an introduction by E.F. Bleiler. Adventures of Old King Brady, Frank James, Nick Carter, Deadwood Dick, Buffalo Bill, The Steam Man, Frank Merriwell, and Horatio Alger — 1877 to 1905. Important, entertaining popular literature in facsimile reprint, with original covers. 190pp. 9 x 12. 22975-0 Pa. $3.50

ALICE'S ADVENTURES UNDER GROUND, Lewis Carroll. Facsimile of ms. Carroll gave Alice Liddell in 1864. Different in many ways from final Alice. Handlettered, illustrated by Carroll. Introduction by Martin Gardner. 128pp. 21482-6 Pa. $2.00

ALICE IN WONDERLAND COLORING BOOK, Lewis Carroll. Pictures by John Tenniel. Large-size versions of the famous illustrations of Alice, Cheshire Cat, Mad Hatter and all the others, waiting for your crayons. Abridged text. 36 illustrations. 64pp. 8¼ x 11. 22853-3 Pa. $1.50

AVENTURES D'ALICE AU PAYS DES MERVEILLES, Lewis Carroll. Bué's translation of "Alice" into French, supervised by Carroll himself. Novel way to learn language. (No English text.) 42 Tenniel illustrations. 196pp. 22836-3 Pa. $3.00

MYTHS AND FOLK TALES OF IRELAND, Jeremiah Curtin. 11 stories that are Irish versions of European fairy tales and 9 stories from the Fenian cycle — 20 tales of legend and magic that comprise an essential work in the history of folklore. 256pp. 22430-9 Pa. $3.00

EAST O' THE SUN AND WEST O' THE MOON, George W. Dasent. Only full edition of favorite, wonderful Norwegian fairytales — Why the Sea is Salt, Boots and the Troll, etc. — with 77 illustrations by Kittelsen & Werenskiöld. 418pp. 22521-6 Pa. $4.50

PERRAULT'S FAIRY TALES, Charles Perrault and Gustave Doré. Original versions of Cinderella, Sleeping Beauty, Little Red Riding Hood, etc. in best translation, with 34 wonderful illustrations by Gustave Doré. 117pp. 8⅛ x 11. 22311-6 Pa. $2.50

EARLY NEW ENGLAND GRAVESTONE RUBBINGS, Edmund V. Gillon, Jr. 43 photographs, 226 rubbings show heavily symbolic, macabre, sometimes humorous primitive American art. Up to early 19th century. 207pp. 8⅜ x 11¼.

21380-3 Pa. $4.00

L.J.M. DAGUERRE: THE HISTORY OF THE DIORAMA AND THE DAGUERREOTYPE, Helmut and Alison Gernsheim. Definitive account. Early history, life and work of Daguerre; discovery of daguerreotype process; diffusion abroad; other early photography. 124 illustrations. 226pp. 6⅙ x 9¼.   22290-X Pa. $4.00

PHOTOGRAPHY AND THE AMERICAN SCENE, Robert Taft. The basic book on American photography as art, recording form, 1839-1889. Development, influence on society, great photographers, types (portraits, war, frontier, etc.), whatever else needed. Inexhaustible. Illustrated with 322 early photos, daguerreotypes, tintypes, stereo slides, etc. 546pp. 6⅛ x 9¼.   21201-7 Pa. **$6.00**

PHOTOGRAPHIC SKETCHBOOK OF THE CIVIL WAR, Alexander Gardner. Reproduction of 1866 volume with 100 on-the-field photographs: Manassas, Lincoln on battlefield, slave pens, etc. Introduction by E.F. Bleiler. 224pp. 10¾ x 9.

22731-6 Pa. **$6.00**

THE MOVIES: A PICTURE QUIZ BOOK, Stanley Appelbaum & Hayward Cirker. Match stars with their movies, name actors and actresses, test your movie skill with 241 stills from 236 great movies, 1902-1959. Indexes of performers and films. 128pp. 8⅜ x 9¼.   20222-4 Pa. $3.00

THE TALKIES, Richard Griffith. Anthology of features, articles from Photoplay, 1928-1940, reproduced complete. Stars, famous movies, technical features, fabulous ads, etc.; Garbo, Chaplin, King Kong, Lubitsch, etc. 4 color plates, scores of illustrations. 327pp. 8⅜ x 11¼.   22762-6 Pa. $6.95

THE MOVIE MUSICAL FROM VITAPHONE TO "42ND STREET," edited by Miles Kreuger. Relive the rise of the movie musical as reported in the pages of Photoplay magazine (1926-1933): every movie review, cast list, ad, and record review; every significant feature article, production still, biography, forecast, and gossip story. Profusely illustrated. 367pp. 8⅜ x 11¼.   23154-2 Pa. $7.95

JOHANN SEBASTIAN BACH, Philipp Spitta. Great classic of biography, musical commentary, with hundreds of pieces analyzed. Also good for Bach's contemporaries. 450 musical examples. Total of 1799pp.

EUK 22278-0, 22279-9 Clothbd., Two vol. set $25.00

BEETHOVEN AND HIS NINE SYMPHONIES, Sir George Grove. Thorough history, analysis, commentary on symphonies and some related pieces. For either beginner or advanced student. 436 musical passages. 407pp.   20334-4 Pa. $4.00

MOZART AND HIS PIANO CONCERTOS, Cuthbert Girdlestone. The only full-length study. Detailed analyses of all 21 concertos, sources; 417 musical examples. 509pp.   21271-8 Pa. **$6.00**

THE FITZWILLIAM VIRGINAL BOOK, edited by J. Fuller Maitland, W.B. Squire. Famous early 17th century collection of keyboard music, 300 works by Morley, Byrd, Bull, Gibbons, etc. Modern notation. Total of 938pp. 8³/₈ x 11.
ECE 21068-5, 21069-3 Pa., Two vol. set $15.00

COMPLETE STRING QUARTETS, Wolfgang A. Mozart. Breitkopf and Härtel edition. All 23 string quartets plus alternate slow movement to K156. Study score. 277pp. 9³/₈ x 12¼.
22372-8 Pa. $6.00

COMPLETE SONG CYCLES, Franz Schubert. Complete piano, vocal music of Die Schöne Müllerin, Die Winterreise, Schwanengesang. Also Drinker English singing translations. Breitkopf and Härtel edition. 217pp. 9³/₈ x 12¼.
22649-2 Pa. $5.00

THE COMPLETE PRELUDES AND ETUDES FOR PIANOFORTE SOLO, Alexander Scriabin. All the preludes and etudes including many perfectly spun miniatures. Edited by K.N. Igumnov and Y.I. Mil'shteyn. 250pp. 9 x 12.
22919-X Pa. $6.00

TRISTAN UND ISOLDE, Richard Wagner. Full orchestral score with complete instrumentation. Do not confuse with piano reduction. Commentary by Felix Mottl, great Wagnerian conductor and scholar. Study score. 655pp. 8¹/₈ x 11.
22915-7 Pa. $11.95

FAVORITE SONGS OF THE NINETIES, ed. Robert Fremont. Full reproduction, including covers, of 88 favorites: Ta-Ra-Ra-Boom-De-Aye, The Band Played On, Bird in a Gilded Cage, Under the Bamboo Tree, After the Ball, etc. 401pp. 9 x 12.
EBE 21536-9 Pa. $6.95

SOUSA'S GREAT MARCHES IN PIANO TRANSCRIPTION: ORIGINAL SHEET MUSIC OF 23 WORKS, John Philip Sousa. Selected by Lester S. Levy. Playing edition includes: The Stars and Stripes Forever, The Thunderer, The Gladiator, King Cotton, Washington Post, much more. 24 illustrations. 111pp. 9 x 12.
USO 23132-1 Pa. $3.50

CLASSIC PIANO RAGS, selected with an introduction by Rudi Blesh. Best ragtime music (1897-1922) by Scott Joplin, James Scott, Joseph F. Lamb, Tom Turpin, 9 others. Printed from best original sheet music, plus covers. 364pp. 9 x 12.
EBE 20469-3 Pa. $7.50

ANALYSIS OF CHINESE CHARACTERS, C.D. Wilder, J.H. Ingram. 1000 most important characters analyzed according to primitives, phonetics, historical development. Traditional method offers mnemonic aid to beginner, intermediate student of Chinese, Japanese. 365pp.
23045-7 Pa. $4.00

MODERN CHINESE: A BASIC COURSE, Faculty of Peking University. Self study, classroom course in modern Mandarin. Records contain phonetics, vocabulary, sentences, lessons. 249 page book contains all recorded text, translations, grammar, vocabulary, exercises. Best course on market. 3 12" 33¹/₃ monaural records, book, album.
98832-5 Set $12.50

MANUAL OF THE TREES OF NORTH AMERICA, Charles S. Sargent. The basic survey of every native tree and tree-like shrub, 717 species in all. Extremely full descriptions, information on habitat, growth, locales, economics, etc. Necessary to every serious tree lover. Over 100 finding keys. 783 illustrations. Total of 986pp.
20277-1, 20278-X Pa., Two vol. set $9.00

BIRDS OF THE NEW YORK AREA, John Bull. Indispensable guide to more than 400 species within a hundred-mile radius of Manhattan. Information on range, status, breeding, migration, distribution trends, etc. Foreword by Roger Tory Peterson. 17 drawings; maps. 540pp.
23222-0 Pa. $6.00

THE SEA-BEACH AT EBB-TIDE, Augusta Foote Arnold. Identify hundreds of marine plants and animals: algae, seaweeds, squids, crabs, corals, etc. Descriptions cover food, life cycle, size, shape, habitat. Over 600 drawings. 490pp.
21949-6 Pa. $5.00

THE MOTH BOOK, William J. Holland. Identify more than 2,000 moths of North America. General information, precise species descriptions. 623 illustrations plus 48 color plates show almost all species, full size. 1968 edition. Still the basic book. Total of 551pp. 6½ x 9¼.
21948-8 Pa. $6.00

HOW INDIANS USE WILD PLANTS FOR FOOD, MEDICINE & CRAFTS, Frances Densmore. Smithsonian, Bureau of American Ethnology report presents wealth of material on nearly 200 plants used by Chippewas of Minnesota and Wisconsin. 33 plates plus 122pp. of text. 6⅛ x 9¼.
23019-8 Pa. $2.50

OLD NEW YORK IN EARLY PHOTOGRAPHS, edited by Mary Black. Your only chance to see New York City as it was 1853-1906, through 196 wonderful photographs from N.Y. Historical Society. Great Blizzard, Lincoln's funeral procession, great buildings. 228pp. 9 x 12.
22907-6 Pa. $6.95

THE AMERICAN REVOLUTION, A PICTURE SOURCEBOOK, John Grafton. Wonderful Bicentennial picture source, with 411 illustrations (contemporary and 19th century) showing battles, personalities, maps, events, flags, posters, soldier's life, ships, etc. all captioned and explained. A wonderful browsing book, supplement to other historical reading. 160pp. 9 x 12.
23226-3 Pa. $4.00

PERSONAL NARRATIVE OF A PILGRIMAGE TO AL-MADINAH AND MECCAH, Richard Burton. Great travel classic by remarkably colorful personality. Burton, disguised as a Moroccan, visited sacred shrines of Islam, narrowly escaping death. Wonderful observations of Islamic life, customs, personalities. 47 illustrations. Total of 959pp.
21217-3, 21218-1 Pa., Two vol. set $10.00

INCIDENTS OF TRAVEL IN CENTRAL AMERICA, CHIAPAS, AND YUCATAN, John L. Stephens. Almost single-handed discovery of Maya culture; exploration of ruined cities, monuments, temples; customs of Indians. 115 drawings. 892pp.
22404-X, 22405-8 Pa., Two vol. set $9.00

CONSTRUCTION OF AMERICAN FURNITURE TREASURES, Lester Margon. 344 detail drawings, complete text on constructing exact reproductions of 38 early American masterpieces: Hepplewhite sideboard, Duncan Phyfe drop-leaf table, mantel clock, gate-leg dining table, Pa. German cupboard, more. 38 plates. 54 photographs. 168pp. 8⅜ x 11¼. 23056-2 Pa. $4.00

JEWELRY MAKING AND DESIGN, Augustus F. Rose, Antonio Cirino. Professional secrets revealed in thorough, practical guide: tools, materials, processes; rings, brooches, chains, cast pieces, enamelling, setting stones, etc. Do not confuse with skimpy introductions: beginner can use, professional can learn from it. Over 200 illustrations. 306pp. 21750-7 Pa. $3.00

METALWORK AND ENAMELLING, Herbert Maryon. Generally coneeded best all-around book. Countless trade secrets: materials, tools, soldering, filigree, setting, inlay, niello, repoussé, casting, polishing, etc. For beginner or expert. Author was foremost British expert. 330 illustrations. 335pp. 22702-2 Pa. $4.00

WEAVING WITH FOOT-POWER LOOMS, Edward F. Worst. Setting up a loom, beginning to weave, constructing equipment, using dyes, more, plus over 285 drafts of traditional patterns including Colonial and Swedish weaves. More than 200 other figures. For beginning and advanced. 275pp. 8¾ x 6⅜. 23064-3 Pa. $4.50

WEAVING A NAVAJO BLANKET, Gladys A. Reichard. Foremost anthropologist studied under Navajo women, reveals every step in process from wool, dyeing, spinning, setting up loom, designing, weaving. Much history, symbolism. With this book you could make one yourself. 97 illustrations. 222pp. 22992-0 Pa. $3.00

NATURAL DYES AND HOME DYEING, Rita J. Adrosko. Use natural ingredients: bark, flowers, leaves, lichens, insects etc. Over 135 specific recipes from historical sources for cotton, wool, other fabrics. Genuine premodern handicrafts. 12 illustrations. 160pp. 22688-3 Pa. $2.00

DRIED FLOWERS, Sarah Whitlock and Martha Rankin. Concise, clear, practical guide to dehydration, glycerinizing, pressing plant material, and more. Covers use of silica gel. 12 drawings. Originally titled "New Techniques with Dried Flowers." 32pp. 21802-3 Pa. $1.00

THOMAS NAST: CARTOONS AND ILLUSTRATIONS, with text by Thomas Nast St. Hill. Father of American political cartooning. Cartoons that destroyed Tweed Ring; inflation, free love, church and state; original Republican elephant and Democratic donkey; Santa Claus; more. 117 illustrations. 146pp. 9 x 12.
22983-1 Pa. $4.00
23067-8 Clothbd. $8.50

FREDERIC REMINGTON: 173 DRAWINGS AND ILLUSTRATIONS. Most famous of the Western artists, most responsible for our myths about the American West in its untamed days. Complete reprinting of *Drawings of Frederic Remington* (1897), plus other selections. 4 additional drawings in color on covers. 140pp. 9 x 12.
20714-5 Pa. $5.00

How to Solve Chess Problems, Kenneth S. Howard. Practical suggestions on problem solving for very beginners. 58 two-move problems, 46 3-movers, 8 4-movers for practice, plus hints. 171pp. 20748-X Pa. $3.00

A Guide to Fairy Chess, Anthony Dickins. 3-D chess, 4-D chess, chess on a cylindrical board, reflecting pieces that bounce off edges, cooperative chess, retrograde chess, maximummers, much more. Most based on work of great Dawson. Full handbook, 100 problems. 66pp. 7⅞ x 10¾. 22687-5 Pa. $2.00

Win at Backgammon, Millard Hopper. Best opening moves, running game, blocking game, back game, tables of odds, etc. Hopper makes the game clear enough for anyone to play, and win. 43 diagrams. 111pp. 22894-0 Pa. $1.50

Bidding a Bridge Hand, Terence Reese. Master player "thinks out loud" the binding of 75 hands that defy point count systems. Organized by bidding problem—no-fit situations, overbidding, underbidding, cueing your defense, etc. 254pp. EBE 22830-4 Pa. $3.00

The Precision Bidding System in Bridge, C.C. Wei, edited by Alan Truscott. Inventor of precision bidding presents average hands and hands from actual play, including games from 1969 Bermuda Bowl where system emerged. 114 exercises. 116pp. 21171-1 Pa. $2.25

Learn Magic, Henry Hay. 20 simple, easy-to-follow lessons on magic for the new magician: illusions, card tricks, silks, sleights of hand, coin manipulations, escapes, and more —all with a minimum amount of equipment. Final chapter explains the great stage illusions. 92 illustrations. 285pp. 21238-6 Pa. $2.95

The New Magician's Manual, Walter B. Gibson. Step-by-step instructions and clear illustrations guide the novice in mastering 36 tricks; much equipment supplied on 16 pages of cut-out materials. 36 additional tricks. 64 illustrations. 159pp. 6⅝ x 10. 23113-5 Pa. $3.00

Professional Magic for Amateurs, Walter B. Gibson. 50 easy, effective tricks used by professionals —cards, string, tumblers, handkerchiefs, mental magic, etc. 63 illustrations. 223pp. 23012-0 Pa. $2.50

Card Manipulations, Jean Hugard. Very rich collection of manipulations; has taught thousands of fine magicians tricks that are really workable, eye-catching. Easily followed, serious work. Over 200 illustrations. 163pp. 20539-8 Pa. $2.00

Abbott's Encyclopedia of Rope Tricks for Magicians, Stewart James. Complete reference book for amateur and professional magicians containing more than 150 tricks involving knots, penetrations, cut and restored rope, etc. 510 illustrations. Reprint of 3rd edition. 400pp. 23206-9 Pa. $3.50

The Secrets of Houdini, J.C. Cannell. Classic study of Houdini's incredible magic, exposing closely-kept professional secrets and revealing, in general terms, the whole art of stage magic. 67 illustrations. 279pp. 22913-0 Pa. $3.00

THE MAGIC MOVING PICTURE BOOK, Bliss, Sands & Co. The pictures in this book move! Volcanoes erupt, a house burns, a serpentine dancer wiggles her way through a number. By using a specially ruled acetate screen provided, you can obtain these and 15 other startling effects. Originally "The Motograph Moving Picture Book." 32pp. 8¼ x 11.　　　　　　　　23224-7 Pa. $1.75

STRING FIGURES AND HOW TO MAKE THEM, Caroline F. Jayne. Fullest, clearest instructions on string figures from around world: Eskimo, Navajo, Lapp, Europe, more. Cats cradle, moving spear, lightning, stars. Introduction by A.C. Haddon. 950 illustrations. 407pp.　　　　　　　　20152-X Pa. $3.50

PAPER FOLDING FOR BEGINNERS, William D. Murray and Francis J. Rigney. Clearest book on market for making origami sail boats, roosters, frogs that move legs, cups, bonbon boxes. 40 projects. More than 275 illustrations. Photographs. 94pp.　　　　　　　　20713-7 Pa $1.50

INDIAN SIGN LANGUAGE, William Tomkins. Over 525 signs developed by Sioux, Blackfoot, Cheyenne, Arapahoe and other tribes. Written instructions and diagrams: how to make words, construct sentences. Also 290 pictographs of Sioux and Ojibway tribes. 111pp. 6⅛ x 9¼.　　　　　　　　22029-X Pa. $1.75

BOOMERANGS: HOW TO MAKE AND THROW THEM, Bernard S. Mason. Easy to make and throw, dozens of designs: cross-stick, pinwheel, boomabird, tumblestick, Australian curved stick boomerang. Complete throwing instructions. All safe. 99pp.　　　　　　　　23028-7 Pa. $1.75

25 KITES THAT FLY, Leslie Hunt. Full, easy to follow instructions for kites made from inexpensive materials. Many novelties. Reeling, raising, designing your own. 70 illustrations. 110pp.　　　　　　　　22550-X Pa. $1.50

TRICKS AND GAMES ON THE POOL TABLE, Fred Herrmann. 79 tricks and games, some solitaires, some for 2 or more players, some competitive; mystifying shots and throws, unusual carom, tricks involving cork, coins, a hat, more. 77 figures. 95pp.　　　　　　　　21814-7 Pa. $1.50

WOODCRAFT AND CAMPING, Bernard S. Mason. How to make a quick emergency shelter, select woods that will burn immediately, make do with limited supplies, etc. Also making many things out of wood, rawhide, bark, at camp. Formerly titled Woodcraft. 295 illustrations. 580pp.　　　　　　　　21951-8 Pa. $4.00

AN INTRODUCTION TO CHESS MOVES AND TACTICS SIMPLY EXPLAINED, Leonard Barden. Informal intermediate introduction: reasons for moves, tactics, openings, traps, positional play, endgame. Isolates patterns. 102pp. USO 21210-6 Pa. $1.35

LASKER'S MANUAL OF CHESS, Dr. Emanuel Lasker. Great world champion offers very thorough coverage of all aspects of chess. Combinations, position play, openings, endgame, aesthetics of chess, philosophy of struggle, much more. Filled with analyzed games. 390pp.　　　　　　　　20640-8 Pa. $4.00

SLEEPING BEAUTY, illustrated by Arthur Rackham. Perhaps the fullest, most delightful version ever, told by C.S. Evans. Rackham's best work. 49 illustrations. 110pp. 7⅞ x 10¾.   22756-1 Pa. $2.00

THE WONDERFUL WIZARD OF OZ, L. Frank Baum. Facsimile in full color of America's finest children's classic. Introduction by Martin Gardner. 143 illustrations by W.W. Denslow. 267pp.   20691-2 Pa. $3.50

GOOPS AND HOW TO BE THEM, Gelett Burgess. Classic tongue-in-cheek masquerading as etiquette book. 87 verses, 170 cartoons as Goops demonstrate virtues of table manners, neatness, courtesy, more. 88pp. 6½ x 9¼.
                                                              22233-0 Pa. $2.00

THE BROWNIES, THEIR BOOK, Palmer Cox. Small as mice, cunning as foxes, exuberant, mischievous, Brownies go to zoo, toy shop, seashore, circus, more. 24 verse adventures. 266 illustrations. 144pp. 6⅝ x 9¼.   21265-3 Pa. $2.50

BILLY WHISKERS: THE AUTOBIOGRAPHY OF A GOAT, Frances Trego Montgomery. Escapades of that rambunctious goat. Favorite from turn of the century America. 24 illustrations. 259pp.   22345-0 Pa. $2.75

THE ROCKET BOOK, Peter Newell. Fritz, janitor's kid, sets off rocket in basement of apartment house; an ingenious hole punched through every page traces course of rocket. 22 duotone drawings, verses. 48pp. 6⅞ x 8⅜.   22044-3 Pa. $1.50

CUT AND COLOR PAPER MASKS, Michael Grater. Clowns, animals, funny faces . . . simply color them in, cut them out, and put them together, and you have 9 paper masks to play with and enjoy. Complete instructions. Assembled masks shown in full color on the covers. 32pp. 8¼ x 11.   23171-2 Pa. $1.50

THE TALE OF PETER RABBIT, Beatrix Potter. The inimitable Peter's terrifying adventure in Mr. McGregor's garden, with all 27 wonderful, full-color Potter illustrations. 55pp. 4¼ x 5½.   USO 22827-4 Pa. $1.00

THE TALE OF MRS. TIGGY-WINKLE, Beatrix Potter. Your child will love this story about a very special hedgehog and all 27 wonderful, full-color Potter illustrations. 57pp. 4¼ x 5½.   USO 20546-0 Pa. $1.00

THE TALE OF BENJAMIN BUNNY, Beatrix Potter. Peter Rabbit's cousin coaxes him back into Mr. McGregor's garden for a whole new set of adventures. A favorite with children. All 27 full-color illustrations. 59pp. 4¼ x 5½.
                                                              USO 21102-9 Pa. $1.00

THE MERRY ADVENTURES OF ROBIN HOOD, Howard Pyle. Facsimile of original (1883) edition, finest modern version of English outlaw's adventures. 23 illustrations by Pyle. 296pp. 6½ x 9¼.   22043-5 Pa. $4.00

TWO LITTLE SAVAGES, Ernest Thompson Seton. Adventures of two boys who lived as Indians; explaining Indian ways, woodlore, pioneer methods. 293 illustrations. 286pp.   20985-7 Pa. $3.50

HOUDINI ON MAGIC, Harold Houdini. Edited by Walter Gibson, Morris N. Young. How he escaped; exposés of fake spiritualists; instructions for eye-catching tricks; other fascinating material by and about greatest magician. 155 illustrations. 280pp. 20384-0 Pa. $2.75

HANDBOOK OF THE NUTRITIONAL CONTENTS OF FOOD, U.S. Dept. of Agriculture. Largest, most detailed source of food nutrition information ever prepared. Two mammoth tables: one measuring nutrients in 100 grams of edible portion; the other, in edible portion of 1 pound as purchased. Originally titled Composition of Foods. 190pp. 9 x 12. 21342-0 Pa. $4.00

COMPLETE GUIDE TO HOME CANNING, PRESERVING AND FREEZING, U.S. Dept. of Agriculture. Seven basic manuals with full instructions for jams and jellies; pickles and relishes; canning fruits, vegetables, meat; freezing anything. Really good recipes, exact instructions for optimal results. Save a fortune in food. 156 illustrations. 214pp. 6⅛ x 9¼. 22911-4 Pa. $2.50

THE BREAD TRAY, Louis P. De Gouy. Nearly every bread the cook could buy or make: bread sticks of Italy, fruit breads of Greece, glazed rolls of Vienna, everything from corn pone to croissants. Over 500 recipes altogether. including buns, rolls, muffins, scones, and more. 463pp. 23000-7 Pa. $4.00

CREATIVE HAMBURGER COOKERY, Louis P. De Gouy. 182 unusual recipes for casseroles, meat loaves and hamburgers that turn inexpensive ground meat into memorable main dishes: Arizona chili burgers, burger tamale pie, burger stew, burger corn loaf, burger wine loaf, and more. 120pp. 23001-5 Pa. $1.75

LONG ISLAND SEAFOOD COOKBOOK, J. George Frederick and Jean Joyce. Probably the best American seafood cookbook. Hundreds of recipes. 40 gourmet sauces, 123 recipes using oysters alone! All varieties of fish and seafood amply represented. 324pp. 22677-8 Pa. $3.50

THE EPICUREAN: A COMPLETE TREATISE OF ANALYTICAL AND PRACTICAL STUDIES IN THE CULINARY ART, Charles Ranhofer. Great modern classic. 3,500 recipes from master chef of Delmonico's, turn-of-the-century America's best restaurant. Also explained, many techniques known only to professional chefs. 775 illustrations. 1183pp. 6⅝ x 10. 22680-8 Clothbd. $22.50

THE AMERICAN WINE COOK BOOK, Ted Hatch. Over 700 recipes: old favorites livened up with wine plus many more: Czech fish soup, quince soup, sauce Perigueux, shrimp shortcake, filets Stroganoff, cordon bleu goulash, jambonneau, wine fruit cake, more. 314pp. 22796-0 Pa. $2.50

DELICIOUS VEGETARIAN COOKING, Ivan Baker. Close to 500 delicious and varied recipes: soups, main course dishes (pea, bean, lentil, cheese, vegetable, pasta, and egg dishes), savories, stews, whole-wheat breads and cakes, more. 168pp. USO 22834-7 Pa. $2.00

COOKIES FROM MANY LANDS, Josephine Perry. Crullers, oatmeal cookies, chaux au chocolate, English tea cakes, mandel kuchen, Sacher torte, Danish puff pastry, Swedish cookies — a mouth-watering collection of 223 recipes. 157pp.
22832-0 Pa. $2.25

ROSE RECIPES, Eleanour S. Rohde. How to make sauces, jellies, tarts, salads, potpourris, sweet bags, pomanders, perfumes from garden roses; all exact recipes. Century old favorites. 95pp.
22957-2 Pa. $1.75

"OSCAR" OF THE WALDORF'S COOKBOOK, Oscar Tschirky. Famous American chef reveals 3455 recipes that made Waldorf great; cream of French, German, American cooking, in all categories. Full instructions, easy home use. 1896 edition. 907pp. 6⅝ x 9⅜.
20790-0 Clothbd. $15.00

JAMS AND JELLIES, May Byron. Over 500 old-time recipes for delicious jams, jellies, marmalades, preserves, and many other items. Probably the largest jam and jelly book in print. Originally titled May Byron's Jam Book. 276pp.
USO 23130-5 Pa. $3.50

MUSHROOM RECIPES, André L. Simon. 110 recipes for everyday and special cooking. Champignons à la grecque, sole bonne femme, chicken liver croustades, more; 9 basic sauces, 13 ways of cooking mushrooms. 54pp.
USO 20913-X Pa. $1.25

THE BUCKEYE COOKBOOK, Buckeye Publishing Company. Over 1,000 easy-to-follow, traditional recipes from the American Midwest: bread (100 recipes alone), meat, game, jam, candy, cake, ice cream, and many other categories of cooking. 64 illustrations. From 1883 enlarged edition. 416pp.
23218-2 Pa. $4.00

TWENTY-TWO AUTHENTIC BANQUETS FROM INDIA, Robert H. Christie. Complete, easy-to-do recipes for almost 200 authentic Indian dishes assembled in 22 banquets. Arranged by region. Selected from Banquets of the Nations. 192pp.
23200-X Pa. $2.50

Prices subject to change without notice.
Available at your book dealer or write for free catalogue to Dept. GI, Dover Publications, Inc., 180 Varick St., N.Y., N.Y. 10014. Dover publishes more than 150 books each year on science, elementary and advanced mathematics, biology, music, art, literary history, social sciences and other areas.